Endless Obsession

King of Ruin
Book Three

Julia Sykes

Copyright © 2024 by Julia Sykes

All rights reserved.

No part of this book may be reproduced in any form or by any electronic or mechanical means, including information storage and retrieval systems, without written permission from the author, except for the use of brief quotations in a book review.

Cover Design by Mayhem Cover Creations

For Dr. B.
Thank you for explaining why I shouldn't use "topolino".

Chapter 1

Massimo

Gunfire popped around me in a deafening, staccato beat. Carmen was shouting something at me, but I couldn't focus on the words. All I could see was the blood staining Evelyn's gold dress, blooming on the pale fabric like a gory rose.

For a moment, my mother's frail, broken body shimmered before me, layering over the waking nightmare. Her blood had spilled over her sunshine yellow dress, and her caramel eyes had been wide with horror as the light faded from them.

My violent impulses had led to her death—if I hadn't tried to join the gang, the boys wouldn't have been provoked into terrorizing my parents.

Now, my fragile little butterfly was bleeding out

in my arms. Because I'd trapped her in my violent world and refused to let her go. She'd told me so many times that she wanted to return to the safety of her mundane life in Albuquerque. But I'd selfishly kept her against her will and coerced her into staying, manipulating her with ruthless pleasure.

"Evelyn..." I murmured her name over and over again, but her eyes remained closed, her face disturbingly serene. The beautiful pink flush that I loved so much had drained from her pale cheeks, her light dusting of freckles standing out in sharp relief against her porcelain complexion.

The gunfire slowed, the shots becoming more infrequent. Whoever had been firing an automatic weapon from the ground floor of Stefano's club must've run out of ammo or been killed. His men were still shooting from the mezzanine level, mowing down whoever was left from the assault team. *Los Zetas* had been fools to think they could take on Stefano Duarte in his own home, no matter how brutal their tactics.

Panicked shouts sounded from below, rapid fire Spanish curses and shouts to retreat.

"I want at least one of them alive," Carmen barked, the cold cartel queen thirsty for vengeance. Stefano was at her side, both of them hovering near us. He caged his wife in a protective embrace. His body shielded hers, the gun in his hand held as naturally as an extension of his arm.

"Call the doctor!" she instructed him. "Evelyn was hit."

My heart twisted at the panic-stricken words. The woman I loved had been shot. Her breaths were shallow, the pulse at her throat weak and sluggish.

I loved Evelyn. I loved her, and now she might die.

Everyone I'd ever loved had been murdered. Because of me.

The fight was over, but the ruined club hadn't gone quiet. A car horn blared from downstairs; *Los Zetas* had rammed their way through the entrance with an armored SUV, and the wrecked vehicle wailed in protest. Glass crunched beneath the quick footsteps of Stefano's guests as they scrambled to capture their wounded enemies before they could flee. And the deep pulse of the club music still thrummed through the darkened space. Golden lights flashed over the blood-splattered dancefloor, a macabre celebration of violence.

The thin, darkhaired man I recognized as Stefano's private physician appeared at my side, his black brows drawn low over his round glasses. "Let me see her."

It took all of my willpower to unlock my arms and lay her down on the floor so that the doctor could inspect her wound. He went to work, cutting her silky dress to reveal the wound at her side. The sight of her blood turned my stomach, and I swallowed down the bile that burned the back of my throat.

"Will she make it?" My question was little more than a strangled rasp.

"I'll do what I can for her," the doctor replied, calm and clinical.

"Save her," I demanded, a savage snarl.

He would die if he failed.

He didn't glance at me; he simply continued to treat her wound. "If you want to distract me with threats, I'm going to have to ask you to leave."

I growled a wordless refusal. I wouldn't leave her side for any reason. I wasn't going anywhere until my broken little butterfly opened her eyes and looked at me with complete devotion. She would promise me that she belonged to me, and she would never leave me.

The thought tormented me. She'd been shot

because of her proximity to me. I should let her go, send her back to her safe life in America.

I wasn't sure if I was strong enough to bear it. The prospect of being separated from her made my stomach twist into knots.

If Evelyn survived, I would do anything to ensure her safety, even if that meant letting her go.

Chapter 2

Evelyn

I drifted in a cottony haze, vacillating between dull pain and weightless bliss. Every time the pain began to crest, warmth suffused my system, cocooning me in peace. Silver eyes filled my dreams, watching over me. Massimo's deep voice rumbled through my disjointed thoughts, soothing me in low, steady streams of Italian. I couldn't understand the words, but the cadence comforted me. His big hand was warm on mine, tethering me to him.

During short periods of lucidity, he filled my world, his comforting scent enfolding me.

"You need to eat, *farfallina*." His strong arm wrapped around me, and my back was propped against his hard chest. I could feel his steady heartbeat, and mine matched it, beating in tandem.

His other hand lifted a chunk of melon to my lips, and I parted them to accept the sweet fruit. My eyelids were so heavy, so I allowed them to drift closed as I released a low hum of contentment. Dull pain still throbbed near my right hip, but I was in Massimo's firm but careful embrace. I loved when he held me like this: like I was precious and delicate. A treasure to be cherished.

"Good girl," he murmured as I ate from his hand. "You're doing so well, *dolcezza*."

His praise warmed my chest, and I sank into him with a sigh. Nothing bad could touch me while Massimo held me. Even the pain ebbed, receding to a soft twinge.

I finished the meal with his low, coaxing words rumbling over me, and then I drifted down into sleep again.

His arms were around me, lifting me. I hissed a pained breath as the movement jarred my hip, and he shushed me gently. He cradled me against his chest and carried me, his steps steady and sure, careful not to jostle me.

The cool tub replaced the heat of his body, but his big hands didn't stray from my skin. He maintained tender contact, stroking and reassuring. Warm water cascaded over my hair, the weight like a gentle massage that eased all tension from my muscles. I relaxed against the tub and tipped my head back, allowing the weight of it to fall into his hands as he lathered my hair with shampoo.

"That's it," he encouraged. "Let me take care of you."

I obeyed, sinking into warm bliss as he rubbed my scalp in soothing circular motions. I trusted him completely, and I knew he would always care for me. I didn't have to worry about anything as long as I was with him.

I stirred, stretching stiff muscles. Pain flared at my hip, a sharp twinge.

But Massimo was holding me, his arm draped around my shoulders and his hand skimming up and down my arm. I released a long breath, and the pain faded.

I blinked up at him, my mind clearer than it had been in...longer than I knew. I wasn't aware of how long I'd been drifting in and out of consciousness.

The last thing I remembered before the hazy days was the violence that'd exploded through Stefano's club. Massimo had raced toward me, his beautiful face a mask of primal fear.

But we weren't in the club. I recognized the bedroom in the opulent suite where Massimo had been staying in Stefano's high rise. We laid on the massive four poster bed where Massimo and I had joined in the most intimate way possible. I was safely cuddled against him. The room was still and quiet, with no sounds of gunfire or shouts of panic.

"What happened?" My voice came out slow and slightly slurred, my mind still a bit fuzzy.

Massimo's jaw ticked, but his touch remained gentle. "You don't need to worry about anything. Just rest."

"But the fight at the club..." People had screamed as they died. Fear punched me, and I jolted in his arms. Ignoring the answering flare of pain, I asked, "Is Carmen okay?"

The cartel queen had been right beside me while the violence unfolded around us.

"Carmen is fine." He reassured me, but his jaw

remained hard as granite. "You need to stay calm. Don't move."

I relaxed against him, obeying without thought. "But what happened?" I asked again. "Was anyone hurt?" My eyes searched his, looking for signs of pain. If my dark savior had been injured…

"*You* were hurt," he almost growled. "You were shot, Evelyn."

Lines of strain appeared around his flashing eyes, but the pain I saw in their depths was for what had happened to me. He hadn't been hurt in the fight.

I breathed a small sigh of relief and trailed my fingers along his jaw to ease the tension away. His rough stubble had grown longer, almost a short beard.

"How long ago?" I asked quietly. My beautiful protector was uncharacteristically disheveled, his glossy black curls untidy, as though he'd run his hand through his hair many times. There were dark circles beneath his eyes, marring his golden skin.

"Ten days," he replied in clipped tones. "I've been managing your pain, but I need you to stay still and focus on recovering. You don't need to worry about anything. I'll take care of you. Get some more sleep. I'll be right here."

I blinked. I'd been mostly unconscious for over a week, and Massimo had been taking care of me. He looked shattered.

"What about you?" I challenged quietly. "Have you slept?"

He turned his face into my hand and kissed my palm. "I'm fine, *dolcezza*."

I tipped my chin back. "I'll sleep if you sleep."

His eyes narrowed with displeasure, not caring for my defiance.

I caressed his cheek, tracing the bold lines of his masculine features until most of the tension melted away. I trailed my fingers through his hair, soothing him the way he'd comforted me.

He released a low sound, something between a hum of contentment and a groan of pain. His eyes closed, and his head dropped back against the pillow.

"*Farfallina...*" he murmured, an exhausted rebuke.

It was my turn to shush him. I was so tired too, drugs still swirling in my system.

I rested my cheek on his chest and relaxed against him. His breathing turned deep and even, and mine slowed to match. We both fell into a peaceful sleep.

The next week passed in a disjointed blur. Massimo insisted that I continue taking painkillers that made me drowsy, and I didn't protest. He wanted me to heal quickly, and I had no reason to argue. The sooner I recovered, the sooner I could stay conscious long enough to have a real conversation with him.

As it was, I spent the days sleeping in his arms, eating from his hand, and being tenderly bathed by him. He saw to my every need, and my whole world centered on him. I was completely reliant on him, and I didn't feel so much as a flicker of disquiet. Being with him felt right, despite my lingering pain. I'd never been cared for like this. No one in my family had taken much notice of me at all while I was growing up, and George had cruelly neglected my needs. He'd insisted that I bend over backward to please him, and nothing I did was ever enough. The point had always been to make me feel small and inadequate, to keep me desperately trying harder to make him happy.

I could see the years of abuse so clearly now that I'd experienced what life could be like with Massimo. He would do anything for me, and he asked for nothing in return. There were no guilt trips or bargaining. He gave me everything I could ever need or desire, and that seemed to make him happy.

I didn't fully understand it—I still didn't feel worthy of such treatment—but I was too addicted to him to question it too closely.

Later into my third week of recovery, Massimo asked me how I'd like to pass the time while I rested. I wanted to know more about him, so I asked what he usually did with his free time.

"I like to read," he replied.

"Really?" I couldn't quite hide my surprise. Massimo was a dangerous man, a man of action. I had a hard time picturing him quietly reading.

He nodded. "My parents wanted me to be educated. They thought that was how I would escape *Le Vele* one day. That dream was never realistic, but they instilled the value of learning in me from a young age. Even after they died, I didn't leave that part of my childhood behind." He absently tucked a stray lock of my hair behind my ear.

"Is that how you honor their memory?" I asked quietly. "By continuing to educate yourself?"

His full lips pressed to a thin line, and he took a moment to consider his answer. "You give me too much credit, *dolcezza*. There was nothing noble about it. Even though my parents were naïve idealists, they were right about one thing: ignorance won't get you very far in life. Gian and Enzo understand that too. When we met at the Camorra bar where we ended up living, we all agreed that we would get out of *Le Vele*. We would use every weapon at our disposal. I was a scrawny kid, and a sharp wit served me better than my fists at the time. My friends and I survived because we were smarter than the other boys. We read everything we could get our hands on."

"What kind of books did you read?" I asked. "Was there a library or something in your neighborhood?"

He snorted his derision. "No, there wasn't a library. We couldn't afford physical books. My shitty old phone was filled with e-books I scoured from the internet. At first, I read up on fighting techniques, then military strategy. But on sleepless nights, I found escape in fiction."

He said it like there had been many sleepless nights. Had he been haunted by nightmares of his parents' murders all throughout his violent childhood?

My heart ached for him, and I tenderly caressed his cheek. He leaned into my gentle touch, as though he couldn't help himself.

"What do you like to read now?" I pressed.

His long fingers trailed through my hair. "Before I came to Mexico City to make this deal with Duarte, I was reading a biography of the emperor Hadrian."

"Do you have it with you?"

His brow furrowed in confusion. "I have the e-book on my phone. Why?"

"Will you read it to me?" My eyelids were feeling heavy again, and I was becoming more aware of the dull ache in my side.

"It's in Italian," he replied.

"I don't mind," I sighed, leaning into him. "I just want to hear your voice."

He dropped a kiss on my forehead. "Anything for you, *farfallina*."

I closed my eyes and allowed his steady stream of rumbling Italian to roll over me, the cadence lilting and almost melodic. Despite the dark circumstances that'd brought me here, there was nowhere else I'd rather be.

"Can we watch something in Italian with English subtitles?" I asked when Massimo turned on the massive TV across from the bed.

"You don't have to do that for me," he replied. "I'm fully fluent in English."

"I know," I said before he could get offended. His English was impeccable. "But I want to learn Italian. I'm good with languages, and I can start picking it up if we put on the subtitles."

His silver eyes shone as they studied my face. "You want to learn Italian?"

I smiled at him. "Yes. If I'm going to Italy with you, I need to speak the language."

His expression shuttered. "I've been thinking about this." The solemn heaviness in his tone made my stomach drop. "You were shot because I kept you here with the cartel. I didn't keep you safe. You were hurt because of your association with me."

My heart twisted, and I grasped his hand in a desperate grip. His words were laced with guilt and something I didn't want to acknowledge. It sounded like a prelude to goodbye.

But I'd committed myself to staying with him before the firefight had broken out in Stefano's club. And now that he'd cared for me so tenderly as I recovered over the last few weeks, I was more attached to my dark savior than ever.

"It wasn't your fault," I said firmly. "George

dragged me into this world when he decided to be on the cartel's payroll. He chose to work for *Los Zetas*. You saved me from them. And from him."

He shook his head, glossy black curls swaying around his gorgeous face. "You said you wanted to go back home to Albuquerque. I refused to let you leave me. You were in the line of fire because of me."

"No," I insisted, clutching him more tightly so that he couldn't put distance between us. "If I'm not with you, George will get to me. He'll kill me to keep his corruption secret. You keep me safe, Massimo."

His lips twisted with regret. "I won't leave you unprotected in Mexico City. But if I send you back to the feds in America, he won't be able to get to you. I was selfish and didn't want to be parted from you, so I kept you." His eyes were dark with pain. "Once you're fully recovered, I'll take you home."

I squared my shoulders, harnessing my defiance to quell the pain in my heart. It wasn't the sting of rejection; it was a keen, cutting sense of loss. I couldn't lose Massimo. I wouldn't allow him to send me away.

"You will take me home," I said evenly. "To Italy. I want to stay with you, Massimo."

He shook his head again, his features drawing

harsh with determination. "That's not your choice. I vowed to protect you, and that means sending you back to Albuquerque. I always keep my promises."

"Then promise me that you won't send me away," I demanded. "Because I don't want to go." I tipped my chin back and allowed my stubborn gaze to clash with his. "Respect my choice, Massimo."

His dark brows drew together. "I do respect you, Evelyn. But I won't put you in danger. My life is dangerous. It always will be. I couldn't live with myself if something happened to you because of me." His cheeks colored with something like shame. "It already has happened. You were shot. I thought you were dying. I can't lose you."

I cupped his cheek. "The only way you'll lose me is if you send me away." I leaned in and brushed a kiss over his taut lips, reassuring him that I was alive and safe in his arms. "I'm right here," I promised. "I'm okay."

"You're hurt," he said gruffly.

"And you're taking care of me," I countered calmly.

"*Farfallina...*" His voice was rough with longing.

"No one has ever taken care of me," I whispered. "I've never let anyone. But I trust you, Massimo. Don't make me go. Please."

He released low sound like a pained groan, and his lips were drawn to mine as though by a magnet. He kissed me like I was made of glass, careful not to jar my injury. I longed for him to sweep me up in a savage kiss and claim me ruthlessly, but I knew I had to recover first. Soon enough, I'd feel him inside me, joining us in the most intimate way possible. Because Massimo wasn't capable of letting me go any more than I was able to leave him. I wasn't sure if I would survive separation, and not just because George still posed a threat to my life. If I lost Massimo, my heart would shatter.

"You don't know what you do to me," he murmured against my lips. "My sweet Evelyn."

"Does this mean you'll teach me Italian?" I asked breathlessly, desperate for his reply.

"Anything for you, *dolcezza*," he vowed. "I'll make sure you feel at home in Naples. I'll show you the kind of life I can provide for you. You will have everything you could ever desire."

I think I already do. I kept the admission locked deep in my chest, afraid that if I declared the intensity of my feelings for him out loud, he might pull away from me again.

No one had ever cared for me like Massimo did. It wasn't the fine gowns or diamonds that made me enamored with him; it was the safety I felt in his strong arms. I could lean on him—I could be vulnerable—and he would never betray my trust in him. It was more than I'd ever dared to dream of.

I sighed and melted against him, conveying everything I couldn't say in an achingly tender kiss.

Chapter 3

Massimo

The man jerked against the ropes that bound him tightly to the metal chair, the only piece of furniture in the dank basement beneath the Camorra bar. Upstairs, Gian and Enzo would be longing for their turn to prove themselves, probably tossing and turning in their makeshift beds in the back room that we'd made our home for the last four years. The brothers were as eager as I was to become *camorrista*. We'd paid our dues and run errands for the Bernardi clan—everything from selling their product on the street to carrying out minor robberies, usually for booze.

Tonight, it was my time to become a man. Their opportunity would come soon enough.

The captive man was rail thin, with visible track marks on his skinny arms. His dirty clothes hung loose on his scrawny frame, but I couldn't see his face. Someone had shoved a black hood over his head, and, judging by the muffled sounds coming from beneath it, he was gagged.

Cesare Salerno loomed behind his captive, cold black eyes glinting with amusement at the man's predicament. His thin lips were stretched into a semblance of a smile, but there was no warmth behind it. In his impeccably tailored suit, he might've passed for a suave gentleman, if you didn't look too closely at his maniacal expression.

We all knew to tread carefully around the notorious sadist and sociopath, who was renowned for making his enemies suffer before they died. He was a powerful man, and one day, he would probably be head of the clan. He was vicious and ruthless, with a cruel streak that made him one of the most feared men in *Le Vele*.

Salerno's dark eyes flashed beneath the spare lightbulb that barely illuminated the concrete space, his inhuman gaze cutting straight into my soul. "I have a job for you, Massimo."

"Anything," I replied eagerly, ready to carry out

any task he demanded of me. This was the first time I'd ever been alone with Salerno—well, alone except for his captive. He'd called me down here, and I'd known that this was my chance to make an impression. To become one of his brothers in blood. I would get out of this shitty bar, out of this shitty neighborhood. Gian and Enzo would get out with me. We'd made a pact, and none of us would leave the others behind.

Salerno fisted the hood and jerked it off his captive's head. Just as I'd suspected, the man was gagged, a dirty length of cloth drawn tightly between his yellowed teeth. Sweat drenched his sun-weathered brow, and his eyes were wild with panic.

"Do you know this man?" Salerno asked.

I studied his fear-twisted features. "No."

Salerno gripped the man's hair, yanking his head back so that I could see his face clearly. "Look at him. Memorize his face. Burn it into your mind."

I nodded, obeying. I studied the dirty man as though he was an insect I would grind beneath my boot.

"You're going to kill him." Salerno's cold command froze the blood in my veins.

My heart stuttered, but I kept my face impassive.

I'd never killed anyone before. I waved a gun around to get people's attention when I needed to, and occasionally, I drew blood with my knife. But I always avoided killing.

My mother's empty, caramel eyes flickered through my mind, the memory of her final look of horror tormenting me.

I straightened my shoulders and faced Salerno.

"Why?" I asked, jerking my chin at the bound man. "What did he do?"

A hint of a smirk played around the corners of Salerno's mouth. He was enjoying this.

"You'll never know. You'll kill him because I ordered you to. Won't you, Massimo?" The last was a snake's challenging hiss.

My mind churned, and I struggled to force down the macabre images of my parents' dead bodies. They'd been innocent, and the gang had gunned them down for no reason.

I'd forsaken my father's pacifism long ago, but the prospect of turning into the same kind of monster who'd murdered him turned my blood cold.

I tipped my chin back and met Salerno squarely in the eye, knowing better than to show a moment of weakness. "And if I don't?"

With the swiftness of a striking viper, he drew

the gun that was holstered at his side. It trained directly on my heart, and I stopped breathing.

"Then you'll die tonight instead."

I swallowed hard, but I kept my shoulders straight. "I don't know this man. Why should I kill him? He hasn't wronged me."

"This isn't about right and wrong," Salerno sneered. "This is about loyalty. This is about doing what you're told. Only one of you is leaving this basement. You get to choose who is breathing when we're finished here. It's you or him. *Camorrista* or death. You want to be one of us, don't you?"

"Yes." My answer was immediate and vehement. I'd longed for this moment of acceptance. I just hadn't realized what I'd have to do to earn it.

"Then prove it," he snapped. "I'm getting bored, and I might just shoot you both if you keep asking stupid questions."

He was still pointing the gun at my chest, but I knew better than to hesitate. I boldly strode toward him, closing the distance between us in smooth strides. I took even breaths and willed my hand not to shake as I lifted it to accept the weapon.

He offered me a savage grin and gave me the gun. My fingers felt numb, but I'd handled a weapon often enough that I could hold it by muscle memory.

I stepped in front of the bound man and pressed the barrel to his forehead, right between his eyes. I could at least make this quick for him.

Because there wasn't a choice at all. This was about more than becoming *camorrista*; this was about survival. And I'd always done what was necessary to survive. Salerno would kill us both if I hesitated. I wasn't willing to end up dead for the kind of foolish principles that'd ruled my father's moral compass. There was no point in both of us dying here tonight.

"Wait."

My heart leapt into my throat. For a moment, I thought I'd passed the test, and Salerno would let us both go.

Then he removed the man's gag.

"Please don't kill me. Please. I have a family. I have three children. They need me to put food on the table. Please, don't do this." The pleas left his bloody lips in a panicked stream. I had no way of knowing if they were true.

He could be lying.

Or his children might starve without him to provide for them.

I glanced at Salerno. For an insane moment, I

considered turning the gun on him and shooting a bullet into his black heart.

But then I would be an enemy of the Camorra. Gian and Enzo would try to protect me, and we'd all be hunted down like dogs. We'd die in the squalor of *Le Vele*, and no one would mourn us.

I wouldn't allow my friends to die because of me.

I looked directly into the bound man's eyes. They were dark green, turned almost black by his dilated pupils. He continued to beg for his life, but his pleas were drowned by the ringing in my ears. I burned his face into my mind. Not because Salerno had commanded it, but because I owed the man that much. I would remember this until the day I died. I would remember him and carry the burden of his death forever. It was a twisted sort of tribute to him, and it was all I could offer.

It took the barest movement of my forefinger to squeeze the trigger. It shouldn't be so easy to kill a man.

I should've used a knife. Having his blood on my hands might've made everything feel more real. I should feel his death in every way possible. Such a violent end should be visceral. And a man should have a chance to defend himself.

I'd shot him right between his eyes and ended his life in less than one of my own selfish heartbeats.

Salerno was laughing quietly. He clapped me on the back and took the gun from my numb fingers.

I followed him out of the basement, leaving the dank space as a man. The half-starved, desperate boy who'd descended these concrete stairs only minutes ago had died in the same instant I'd ended my victim's life. I'd just attained everything I'd ever wanted, and my soul was screaming because of it.

"Massimo." Evelyn's soft voice soothed my wounded soul like a healing balm. "Massimo, wake up."

I buried my face in her silken hair, breathing in her floral scent to ground myself in the present. I wasn't that weak boy anymore. I'd killed plenty more men since that night I became a man. I'd lost count of how many had died by my hand.

But unlike that night, I always killed with a purpose. I had my own code of honor and sense of justice, something that Salerno would never understand. He was my boss now, as cruel and conniving as ever. But Gian, Enzo, and I had become powerful enough that he didn't often command us to cross our own moral lines. Even the most loyal dog would bite if cornered.

We were loyal to our clan, not Salerno personally. But until the day came when we were able to overthrow the bastard, we had to owe him our fealty. The day of reckoning was coming soon now that we'd made this deal with Duarte and Rodríguez.

"What are you thinking?" Evelyn murmured, trailing her soft fingers through my curls. The light scrape of her nails over my scalp sent tingles down my spine. "Tell me about your dream."

I shook my head. I would never tell her about that awful night. There were some darker details about my past that she didn't need to know. She would turn from me in revulsion, and I couldn't bear that.

"Look at me," she cajoled, tugging lightly at my hair.

My eyes locked on hers. They glittered through the darkness of the night, capturing the city lights that shone through the dimmed floor to ceiling window. The stars in her eyes were stunning, hypnotic.

"I'm not a good man," I heard myself confess, the truth drawn from deep in my soul. I'd always known it, but I'd never allowed myself to contemplate it. I was unapologetic of my violent lifestyle because I knew the darker truths of the world.

But my parents would be ashamed of what I'd become. And now, I clung to precious Evelyn with bloodstained hands.

"I can't change what I am. But I will be good to you, *farfallina*. I swear."

She caressed my cheek, and I leaned into the tender touch. "I don't want you to change," she said in a fierce whisper. "I accept who you are, Massimo. All of you."

"You don't know all of me," I admitted.

And she never would. I would shield her from the cruelest aspects of my life.

The stars danced in her eyes. "I've seen who you are. You've shown me so many times. You always do what you think is right. You're loyal to the people you care about, and you protect innocent people. You're not cruel or callous."

"I'm a dangerous man," I warned her.

"I know," she replied evenly. "That doesn't change how I feel about you."

I placed my hand over her heart.

How do you feel about me? I barely kept the question locked in my chest. I loved this woman, and the prospect that she didn't share the depth of my feelings unnerved me. In time, she would love me as I loved her. I wouldn't settle for anything less than soul-deep devotion. She was already addicted to my touch, and I knew she felt affection for me. That was enough for now.

Soon, we would start our new life together in Italy. I would help Gian and Enzo with their coup. And I would be powerful and wealthy enough to keep Evelyn safe and blissfully happy.

She would love me. She didn't have a choice.

Chapter 4

Evelyn

Four Weeks Later

"How is she?" Massimo asked the doctor, his silver eyes dark with worry.

"I feel fine," I promised, drawn to ease his concern. "I haven't felt so much as a twinge of pain for days."

"That's good," the doctor approved before turning his attention to Massimo. "She's made a full recovery. She can return to a normal routine."

I cleared my throat, not caring for how he was addressing Massimo and not me. "Like I said, I feel fine," I reiterated coolly.

The doctor simply nodded. "I'm satisfied that there won't be any lasting damage. Initially, I was concerned about potential fertility issues, but everything has healed nicely. It would be wise to check with your own physician when you get home if you want to do further tests for peace of mind."

My brain tripped over the thought. I'd been shot on my right side, low toward my hip. I'd been informed that the bullet had missed my major organs, but I hadn't thought about my fertility being impacted.

Fear pulsed through me at the prospect that I might not be able to have a family with Massimo.

Did I want to have Massimo's baby? I'd always wanted a child of my own, someone to love unconditionally, the way I'd never been loved.

I took a quick breath and pushed the thought away. It was far too soon to contemplate starting a family with him, no matter how tempting the idea was. Something like yearning tugged at my heart.

I leaned into his chest, wrapping my arms around him so that I could feel his heartbeat beneath my ear. It was the most reassuring sound in the world.

The doctor excused himself discretely, leaving us alone in the bedroom. For a moment, I expected Massimo to sweep me up in a fierce, desperate kiss.

But his phone chimed, shattering the tender moment.

He checked the message and muttered a low curse.

"Is something wrong?" I asked, worry nipping at me.

He stroked my hair. "No, *dolcezza*. We're about to have a visitor."

Fifteen minutes later, Carmen beamed at me as she settled into the plush armchair across from the couch where we were seated.

"It's so good to see you, Evelyn. Massimo has been keeping you well guarded." She shot him an exaggerated pout. "He wouldn't let me visit until today."

He draped his strong arm over me and tucked me close to his side. I leaned into him, sighing in contentment.

"He's been taking good care of me," I told the cartel queen. "I'm all better now."

He dropped a kiss on the top of my head. "You still need to be careful with yourself, *farfallina*."

I grasped his hand and gave it a reassuring squeeze. "The doctor says I'm fine," I reminded him. "Totally healed up."

"I'm glad to hear it," Carmen said with genuine

warmth. "Stefano and I have been very worried with you two shut up in here. We weren't sure if you were on your deathbed since Massimo wouldn't let anyone in to see you."

Another exaggeration and a slight jab at my dark protector. I was sure that the doctor would've kept her informed on my progress; she was his boss. She clearly wasn't pleased that Massimo had been keeping her locked out of a suite in her own home.

But she had allowed us privacy, so she must've sensed that fighting with him would accomplish nothing except upsetting me. Carmen was shrewd as well as caring. She did feel concern for me and possibly something like friendship, but she knew how to navigate tense situations with dangerous men.

"I hope you haven't been too bored," she drawled, another pointed remark.

"Not at all." I defended Massimo. "He's been teaching me Italian. Now, I'll be ready to speak the language when we go to Naples."

Her eyes cut to him. "Are you so keen to go soon?"

A muscle ticked in his jaw for half a second, but he managed a genial smile. "Our business is concluded. Gian and Enzo sent the payment from our end weeks ago. We can all start making money now. It's time for me to go home and oversee the final aspects of our deal."

Her dark brows lifted. "And what about your other business here in Mexico City? I was under the impression that it was unfinished."

I tensed, not caring for their conversation about their criminal empires. Even though I'd accepted this part of Massimo's life, I didn't like hearing the details.

His thumb traced soothing circles on my upper arm, but he kept his glinting gaze fixed on Carmen. "I haven't forgotten about that. I intend to see the job through, but I need to get Evelyn safely to Naples first. I'll come back to tie up the loose end as soon as she's settled."

"What? No," I protested. I couldn't bear to be parted from him. My addiction to him should scare me, but I was too lost in our connection to care. And the prospect of being alone in Naples with his mafia associates unnerved me. "I want to stay with you."

Carmen studied my panicked features. Her crimson-painted lips thinned to a slash as she considered me. Then her sharp gaze cut back to Massimo.

"Go with Evelyn. Stefano and I will handle Crawford."

My heart skipped a beat. *George.* My ex-fiancé was the loose end they were discussing. Massimo and Duarte wanted him dead. The prospect made my stomach churn.

Even though I knew I wouldn't be safe as long as George was alive, having him killed disturbed me. Would I ever become accustomed to this violent world where justice and retribution were dealt out in blood?

"I made a promise," Massimo countered, his thumb still stroking my arm. "I intend to keep it."

Carmen dismissed the notion with a flick of her manicured fingers. "And I'm releasing you from that promise. Besides, Stefano will prefer to handle this personally after the brazen attack on our home. Our new business venture is too important for you to linger here."

"Evelyn won't be safe until I end Crawford."

I shifted against him, but he kept his attention fixed on Carmen. His arm tightened around me slightly, a reassuring embrace. He wouldn't apologize for his intention to eliminate George as a threat, and I didn't expect him to. I understood him well enough now to know that he would do anything to protect me. I had to trust in him if we were going to be together.

"I am more than capable of defending my own territory," Carmen said coolly. "Crawford is a threat. I do not tolerate threats." She tipped her chin in my direction. "Take Evelyn home. I'll call you when it's done."

Home. She was talking about Italy. Naples would be my home now.

My belly fluttered, equal parts trepidation and excitement. I would start a new life with Massimo, but I was also entering the unknown. I would have to rely on him to introduce me to his friends, who were all likely to be criminals. But I knew none of them would ever harm me. I belonged to Massimo.

I leaned into him, conveying my trust and acceptance. I would never make him feel ashamed of who he was. Life had been cruel to him, and he'd done what was necessary to survive.

I'm not a good man. The memory of his anguished words in the wake of his nightmare made my heart squeeze. Massimo might lead a dangerous life, but he wasn't evil. I would remind him of that every day.

"I'll leave you two alone to make plans for your trip," Carmen announced, the matter handled. "I can arrange an overnight flight for you tonight. Will you be ready by then?"

"Yes," Massimo replied. "Thank you, Carmen. I owe you a debt."

She gave an imperious wave of her hand again. "We're friends, Massimo. You don't owe me anything."

She sounded like she meant it. Stefano was cold and calculating, but his wife was softer, if no less formidable.

"Take care, Evelyn." She offered me a warm smile. "Massimo will give you my number, and you can reach out to me at any time."

"Thank you." My throat was strangely tight.

Friends were a rarity in my life. I'd always kept myself emotionally isolated because social situations were safer that way; I couldn't be hurt by anyone's indifference if I didn't allow myself to become attached to them. George had been the one exception, and even then, I'd never allowed myself to rely on him. I'd supported *him*, not the other way around. It hadn't been reciprocal.

A whole new world was opening up before me, and it was all because of Massimo. He'd stormed into my life and shown me that I could be vulnerable. He'd proven to me that he would protect me in every way, including shielding my heart.

Carmen said her goodbye to Massimo too, and then she swept out of the suite, giving us privacy.

"Pick out what clothes you want to take with you," Massimo encouraged, guiding me toward the bedroom. "We can buy more when you get to Naples. I'll take you shopping."

My brows lifted. "You'd go shopping with me?"

His lips curved in a wicked smirk. "I insist. I want to see you try everything on. I like buying pretty things for you."

My cheeks heated, and I barely managed to shrug off my budding lust. "What you've bought for me while we've been staying here in Mexico City is more than enough. I'll just pack it all."

His dark brows drew together in warning. "I thought we had agreed that you would let me spoil you."

Unease stirred in my belly, an echo of lifelong distrust. "When did I agree to that? I love the beautiful clothes that you've bought for me, and I'm grateful for them, but I don't need more. I'm usually very reserved in my style choices, Massimo. This isn't me."

His jaw firmed, and he tipped his chin back in challenge. "Why not? Why can't it be you? Silks and jewels suit you, *farfallina*. My woman deserves the finer things in life. You will have every pretty little thing you desire. Nothing is out of reach for us."

Us. My heart tugged toward his, as though we were connected by an invisible tether.

I closed the short distance between us and wrapped my arms around him, tucking my body close to his. He immediately returned my embrace, both of us craving constant contact.

"Is this still about your stepfather?" he rumbled, a slight edge to the question. I knew the anger was directed at the cruel, callous man who'd raised me. "You said he made you feel like you owed him for providing you with necessities. I will never treat you that way. I swear."

"I know," I promised. I didn't want him to think I doubted his goodness and sincerity. "But it's more than that." The confession was drawn from a place so deep in my soul that I hadn't even consciously known it was lurking at the core of me. "I told you about how my real dad left when I was four," I began. "I should hate him for that, but the few memories I have of him are good.

"One day—about six months before he left—I said I was sick because I wanted to spend time with him. He must've known I wasn't actually sick, but he called out from work and spent the day with me. He took me out for pancakes, and then we went to the zoo. He bought me a stuffed giraffe. I slept with it until I was twelve. My mom found out that I'd kept something he'd given to me, and she threw it away. I felt like she was destroying a part of me, even though I'd thought about burning the thing myself a thousand times."

I shook my head, as though I could toss away the pain of the memories. "Before he abandoned us, I thought he loved me. He doted on me and made me feel special. Like I was the center of his world."

I realized that deep down, I felt unworthy of Massimo's lavish affections because I feared that they wouldn't last. I was terrified of trusting in him only to be abandoned again.

Massimo's big hand cradled my nape, his thick fingers sliding into my hair to hold me firmly. His silver eyes flashed with a fervent light as he stared down at me, as though he was peering straight into my damaged soul.

"I will never abandon you, Evelyn."

The promise pierced my heart, a painfully sweet pledge. Believing him hurt because I had to rip down a lifetime of boundaries, walls I'd put up to protect myself.

But for him, I would make myself vulnerable. I chose to trust in him.

A giddy sensation soared through me, like I'd just jumped off a cliff and was in freefall. I felt wild and a bit reckless, but I knew Massimo would keep me safe from harm. The burden of holding up those walls for so many years dropped away, and I felt almost weightless.

I bracketed his beautiful face with both hands, holding him like he was my own personal treasure. "Thank you."

"There's nothing to thank me for. I'm keeping you because I'm a selfish bastard, and I refuse to let you go. If I were a good man, I'd send you back to America. But it's too late for that now. There's no going back."

He said it like it was something ominous, but I wasn't afraid. And I would prove that to him every day.

"You're *my* good man," I purred, going up onto my toes to press a tender kiss against the grim slash of his lips. "I can't wait to start our lives together in Naples. I can't wait to make it my home too."

I'd been searching for a sense of home ever since my dad had walked out on me, and my simple childhood sense of security had been shattered. I certainly hadn't felt at home in my stepfather's house, and I'd only known further, more insidious torment during my years with George.

I'd never been to Italy, and I barely knew the language, but I felt sure that as long as I was with Massimo, I would find a home. We would make one together.

He looked at me with reverence, his eyes shining with awe. "You are too good for me, *dolcezza*. So sweet and perfect."

My cheeks flushed with pleasure at his words, and the rest of my body heated for him too. He hadn't touched me sexually since I'd been shot, and I'd become steadily needier as the days dragged on.

"I need you, Massimo. Please."

"I don't want to hurt you." His features were tight with his own hunger, a desperate longing that matched my own.

"You won't." I'd never been surer of anything in my life. "You would never hurt me. I trust you. And right now, I need you to touch me." I boldly grasped his hand and dragged it toward my sex. "I'm aching for you."

He sucked in a sharp breath, shocked at my brazen behavior. He pressed his palm against my clit, and I bucked at the first jolt of pleasure after weeks of long denial.

"How can I leave you aching, my sweet girl?" His fingers dipped between my thighs, so that he grasped my pussy in a proprietary hold. "Is this what you want?"

"Yes," I moaned, dropping quick, desperate kisses along his jaw until I nipped at the shell of his ear with a ragged whisper. "Please, Massimo."

He released a low hum that vibrated through my chest and down to my core, making me shudder with mounting desire. "You'll have to be very good for me, *farfallina*. But you always are. You love being my good girl, don't you?"

"Yes," I agreed again, my voice breathy with lust. "I'm your good girl."

He growled his satisfaction and grazed his teeth down my throat, tracing the line of my vulnerable artery. I expected a possessive bite on my shoulder, but he pressed a tender kiss there instead, flicking his tongue over my sensitized skin. Every inch of my body came alive for him, sparks dancing along my heated flesh.

I melted into him, overwhelmed by the rush of carnal sensation. It'd been so long since he'd touched me like this that the sudden onslaught of pleasure was intense enough to make my knees weak. It was almost as though I was experiencing his masterful touch for the first time, our chemistry shockingly potent.

He took his time with me, lavishing me with deep kisses as he slowly eased the lightweight white robe from my shoulders, then stripped off my silky nightgown. When I was naked before him, my body trembled with the force of my desire, and I clung to his corded arms for support.

He stepped toward me, never breaking contact as he guided me toward the bed. He settled me down on the center of the mattress, ensuring my comfort.

I loved when he handled me with harsh, primal passion, but this gentle, careful seduction was sweet enough to make my eyes sting even as my body sang for him.

He brushed one more kiss over my forehead and commanded, "Stay."

I nodded, and he left me briefly to retrieve three lengths of rope from the chest of drawers. My tongue darted out to wet my lips, my body primed for his perverse games. He hadn't bound me in weeks, and I longed to feel his ropes enfolding me once again, restraining me in a secure embrace.

"I'm going to make sure you stay still and don't

strain yourself," he told me as he grasped my ankle and wrapped the rope around it.

I considered protesting again and insisting that I was all healed up, but I knew he needed it to be this way between us. He had to feel thoroughly in control because he'd had to watch me bleed in his arms. Massimo was a powerful man, and the sense of helplessness to save me must've tormented him.

But he'd taken such good care of me while I healed. I would prove to him how much that meant to me by allowing him to bind me without protest. This seduction would be on his terms, and that was how I liked it too. We were perfectly matched, bonded by mutual need and deviant desires.

"I trust you," I promised as he wound the rope around my thigh, bending my knee so that my heel touched the back of my leg.

He bound me in that position, wrapping the rope around my shin to secure me in place. He repeated the process on my other leg. When he was satisfied that my legs were thoroughly immobilized, he grasped my waist and lifted me, positioning me so that I was on my knees before him.

The ropes twisted and sank deeper into my flesh, the tight binding biting into me just hard enough to make me keenly aware of my helplessness to resist anything he wanted to do to me. My legs were spread wide, my swollen sex on lewd display. Desire wet my lower lips, my body primed for him.

He wasn't finished restraining me. The third length of rope encircled my wrists, capturing them so that they pressed together. Once they were securely bound, he tugged on the length, drawing my arms over my head and back down. My elbows bent, and my hands touched my hair at my nape. The position forced my back to arch, offering my breasts to him.

He quickly lashed the rope around my chest, securing my wrists behind my head and trapping me in the vulnerable position.

His full lips tilted in a satisfied smirk, and his eyes darkened with lust. He cupped my breasts, as though he was learning the weight and shape of them all over again. My head dropped back on a low moan, and a warm wave of pleasure rolled through me, emanating from his heated touch.

"*Bellissima.*" His voice was rough with reverence, and he rubbed his calloused fingers over my peaked nipples.

I cried out at the shock of bliss that sparkled in tingling lines from my hard buds to my clit. It pulsed in time with my heartbeat, and my inner muscles contracted, aching to be filled.

"Please," I panted. "Please..."

"Say my name when you beg." The order rumbled through me, drawing a shiver to the surface of my skin.

"Please, Massimo." My plea left me on a desperate whimper as he continued to toy with my breasts, stimulating me without touching me where I needed it most.

"Tell me what you want. I want to hear the filthy words on these sweet lips." He brushed his thumb over my lips, and I licked him, swirling my tongue around his thumb the way I would worship his cock.

He hissed in a sharp breath. "Don't tease me, *farfallina*," he warned.

The dark edge to his words sent a thrill racing through my body, and I submitted to his will.

"Please touch my pussy, Massimo. Let me come. I need you."

"Such a good girl." His praise rolled down my spine like warm honey, pooling low in my belly. "You're doing so well, *dolcezza*." He kissed my forehead, my lips, my neck, and down to the hollow between my collarbones.

I tipped my head back as much as I was able, welcoming him to take more.

"So beautiful in my ropes," he murmured just before his tongue flicked my sensitive nipple.

I cried out at the burst of ecstasy that rocked my body, and his strong arm braced around my waist, caging me in a firm embrace to hold me still.

"Don't struggle," he cooed, his lips teasing my nipple.

I whined in primal need, but I forced myself to remain as still as possible. My instincts told me to writhe and buck against him, seeking more stimulation. But I was caged by his will as firmly as by his ropes. I shook with the effort of holding my most animal urges in check, but I managed to obey him. Pleasing him was the only thing that mattered, my entire body and mind completely devoted to him.

He tormented my breasts with his teeth and tongue, nipping at me with sharp little jolts of pain, quickly soothed away by warm pleasure. One arm remained firmly around my waist while his other hand skimmed down my belly, his thick fingers teasing just above my throbbing clit.

I panted his name and pleaded with him in a litany, a carnal prayer to my beautiful god. My entire world centered on him and the pleasure he wrung from my body, playing me like his favorite instrument.

When he finally touched my clit with the barest brush of his thumb, I cried out and arched into him.

He shushed me gently, a quiet rebuke for my sudden jolting movement. I whimpered and went still, struggling to obey when my entire body was crying out for release.

His low chuckle shuddered through me, his arrogant amusement at my predicament only stoking my need for him as I sank deeper into his control.

As I panted and pleaded with him, he told me how well I was doing, how good I was, how much I pleased him. Each warm affirmation went straight to my head, intoxicating. I felt drunk on his praise, his power over me. My body went taut, and my skin grew slick with the effort of remaining still for him.

"Good girl." Two fingers parted my slick, swollen folds, easing into me with aching care.

My eyes stung at the overwhelming sense of being cherished and filled, his touch both reverent and merciful. He circled my clit with his thumb and crooked his fingertips against the sensitive spot inside me. At the same time, he sucked on my nipple, grazing it with his teeth.

I came apart on a scream, and his restraining arm tightened around me to hold me firmly through my orgasm. Ecstasy wracked my trembling body, shuddering through me with relentless force. I moaned his name and pressed my forehead into his thick black curls, leaning into his strength, relying on him to keep me still when I was spiraling out of control.

"I've got you," he murmured against my chest. "Let go, *farfallina*."

He sucked on my other nipple and continued to stimulate my sex, coaxing more pleasure from my trembling body.

I half-sobbed his name, melting into him and trusting him to hold me while I allowed the bliss to consume me. He continued to stimulate me until my clit became overly sensitive, a light sting of discomfort edging into my pleasure.

When I sucked in a shuddering breath, he withdrew his hand, having mercy on me.

His silver eyes locked on mine, and he lifted his fingers to his full lips. He kept me captive in his lust-darkened stare as he licked at my slick desire that coated his hand. He growled his appreciation and sucked his fingers clean, his remarkable eyes closing in a brief moment of his own bliss.

He claimed my mouth in a devastating kiss, and I tasted myself on his tongue. The act was purely primal, a forceful demonstration of how he'd made me come undone for him. I was wanton in my desire for this beautiful man, my dark savior, and I didn't feel so much as a shred of shame.

The rope shifted around my chest, tugging at my wrists. He was untying me. I relaxed against him, melting as the tight embrace of the ropes loosened, and only his strong arms supported me.

He laid back on the pillows, arranging me over his chest so that my head rested over his heart. The steady beat calmed me, but I glanced up at him in confusion.

"What about you?" My words were slow and slightly lust-drunk.

He tenderly stroked my hair. "Not yet, *dolcezza*. All I want is to take care of you. That's enough to satisfy me. I'm so proud of you. You were so good for me."

I flushed and tucked my face against him, snuggling into his warmth. I breathed in his unique scent of leather and amber, sinking into him.

Somehow, this dangerous, possessive, perfect man was utterly devoted to me. Massimo was all mine, and I'd never been happier in my entire life.

Chapter 5

Massimo

"Take this. It will help you sleep." I pressed a small, round white pill into Evelyn's palm, and she frowned at it.

"I've been sleeping for weeks," she protested.

I brushed a soothing kiss over her brow. "Stefano's jet is comfortable enough, but I want to make sure you get a good night's rest. We'll arrive in Italy at dawn, and it will be easier to adjust to the time change if you sleep through the flight."

We were already somewhere over the Atlantic, finally on our way home. I regretted that I was leaving Mexico City without killing George Crawford myself, but I couldn't deny that getting her away from him and *Los Zetas* calmed me with every passing mile.

Soon, we'd be back in my own territory, and I'd be able to get her settled into my life.

Our lives.

I just needed her to take the drug so that I could rest too. There was one small thing I needed to handle to fully ease my anxiety about her safety, and it would be much easier if she slept while I did what was necessary.

"Okay," she sighed and took the pill.

"Good girl." I kissed her again, pleased at her easy compliance. Evelyn sometimes frustrated me with her defiance, but she never argued without a good reason. I'd learned to respect the moments she chose to challenge me.

"I'd probably be too excited to sleep, anyway," she admitted.

A slow smile stretched my lips. "Are you excited about going to Naples with me?"

Her bright grin hit me like a ray of pure sunshine. "I've always wanted to go to Italy. And now I get to go with you."

"We're not going on vacation," I reminded her. "I'll arrange citizenship papers for you once we arrive."

Marriage to me would be the quickest way to legitimize the paperwork, but now wasn't the time for a proposal. Evelyn deserved something far more romantic, and I would make the moment special for her. I resolved to buy a ring as soon as we landed.

Her brow furrowed. "What about getting through customs?" she asked, as though it had just occurred to her. "George still has my passport."

"Carmen's people made all the necessary arrangements with the border agents. No one will ask us any questions." The right people had been paid to look the other way, and the cartel queen had provided an excellent forged American passport for Evelyn.

More details that she didn't need to worry about. I knew my criminal activities would never sit well with her, so she didn't need to know about the fake documents. I would ensure that our marriage was legal and legitimate when the time came. I would give her every aspect of a normal life that I could provide.

Evelyn blinked slowly, the sleeping pill already making her drowsy. She snuggled into me with a contented sigh. "Tell me about Naples. In Italian, please."

"What do you want to know?"

"Tell me about where we will live." She yawned. "I can't wait to see it."

My chest warmed, and I stroked her silken hair. I

started to describe my home to her—the apartment we would now share. I told her it was too small, so I would buy her someplace bigger. Big enough for a family. We would pick it out together.

By the time I told her about the wealthy, safe neighborhood where we would settle, she was fast asleep in my arms, her breathing deep and even.

I carried her the short distance to the small bedroom at the back of the plane and laid her out on the bed. Then I pulled out the syringe the doctor had discretely given me when he came to the suite for his final visit this morning. I'd asked Stefano to help me acquire what I needed, and my new friend had delivered.

Evelyn didn't so much as stir when I carefully slid the needle into her shoulder and injected the tiny tracking chip.

I breathed a sigh of relief. Now, I would always know exactly where she was. If I had to leave her for my business, I could check her location whenever I started to feel edgy without her.

The night she'd tried to run away from me had been the most awful experience of my life. Not knowing where she was and fearing for her safety had been agony. She'd almost been raped because I hadn't been able to find her fast enough. If I'd arrived at that military outpost even a minute later…

I shoved the bloody memories away, cuddling her close so that I could breathe in her floral scent. It calmed me like nothing else.

She stirred at my side, slowly stretching her lithe body. For a moment, I thought she was waking up, but her eyes remained closed. Her brow furrowed slightly, and her cheeks flushed.

"Massimo…" My name was a low slur, but I understood that lustful tone clearly enough.

I sucked in a deep breath and caught the familiar, alluring scent of her arousal. She pressed her hips against my thigh, slowly grinding against me.

I stroked her hair, trying to calm my own burst of dark lust in response to her wanton actions. "Sleep, *dolcezza*. I'm right here."

Her lashes fluttered, but her eyes remained closed, the drugs keeping her under. She moaned my name again and writhed in my arms.

"Need you…" she murmured, the words barely discernable.

I bit out a soft curse and tried to ignore the way my cock stirred. She was so soft and helpless right now, sleepy and trusting and burning with need for me.

It'd been so long since I'd buried myself inside her and staked my claim over her delicate body. For weeks, all I'd cared about was her wellbeing, ensuring that she was whole and healed. Now, my own body was keenly aware of how long I'd denied myself the pleasure of fucking my pretty little butterfly.

But I couldn't. Not when she was like this.

She whimpered and rocked her hips against me again, the sound almost pained.

"Are you aching again, *farfallina*?" I kissed her furrowed brow. "I'll make it all better."

I couldn't leave her wanting, not when she was clearly desperate for release. I'd given her an orgasm this morning, but she'd been suffering for long weeks without me too. And now that she was fully recovered, her desires were keener than ever.

I pushed her dress up over her thighs, until the soft cotton pooled around her hips. I gently tugged her white lace panties down her long legs, revealing her wet cunt. Fuck, she was slick with need, her pussy swollen and ready for me.

I eased two fingers inside her and rubbed her g-spot, gritting my teeth against my own painful need. This was about her comfort, not slaking my own lust.

"No..."

I stilled immediately, my heart skipping a beat. She didn't consent to this. I had to stop.

"Need you," she slurred again, her lashes fluttering as though she was struggling to wake. "Inside me."

She whimpered my name, and the pained, desperate sound broke me.

"All right, *dolcezza*," I soothed her. "I'll make you feel good."

My cock was painfully hard when I freed it from the confines of my jeans. It jutted toward her wet pussy, and my need to claim her for the first time in weeks drove me close to madness.

She groaned and thrashed, wanton and desperate. My beautiful, helpless little butterfly needed me.

I shushed her gently and lined my cock up with her slick opening. "I'll take care of you, Evelyn. You're safe with me."

She released a long, happy sigh as I eased into her tight pussy, stretching her in an agonizingly slow slide. Her velvet heat squeezed my dick, and I saw stars. I gritted my teeth and forced myself to be gentle when all of my most savage instincts were roaring at me to stake my claim over what was mine. Evelyn belonged to me, and I needed to brand her once again, to remind both of us that she belonged to me in every way.

She wriggled beneath me, so I grasped her wrists and pinned them above her head.

"You don't have to move," I soothed her. "You don't have to do anything except feel the pleasure of me filling you up. Relax, and let me in. I'll give you what you need."

She went limp on a low groan, her inner muscles relaxing around me. I sucked in a breath and harnessed my control, no longer tempted to the edge of orgasm. I would make this good for her. I'd never leave my sweet girl in any sort of discomfort, and the darkest part of me couldn't deny that I liked having her completely at my mercy. I could do anything I wanted to her, and she would welcome it because she trusted me implicitly.

I thrust into her, claiming her in long strokes. Each time my cockhead dragged across her g-spot, she panted out little moans of pleasure. The soft sounds of uncontrolled ecstasy spurred me on, and I began to fuck her in earnest. I nipped at the shell of her ear, kissed my way down her neck, and bit into her shoulder, marking her in the way she liked. Evelyn loved being owned by me, and she would be reassured by my mark when we arrived in Naples.

She cried out at the flare of pain that accompanied my savage bite, and her core contracted. The tight grip of her sheath drove me to the edge, and pleasure gathered at the base of my spine. Keeping her wrists trapped with one hand, I reached between us with the other and tweaked her sensitive nipples.

She made a guttural sound of raw ecstasy, and her pussy milked my cock, stealing the last shreds of my control. I emptied myself inside her on a rough shout, driving deep to fill her up with my cum.

As I came down from the peak, lethargy sapped my muscles, and I collapsed beside her. She went limp against me, her body draped over mine. She no longer whimpered or writhed; her breaths were slow and even, her cheeks still flushed with pleasure.

I closed my eyes and followed her down into deep, blissful sleep.

Chapter 6

Evelyn

I leaned into Massimo with a happy sigh, content despite the fact that I was entering the unknown. The slight soreness between my legs elicited a warm glow in my chest; it was a sweet reminder that he'd finally claimed me for the first time since I'd been shot. My memories of sex on the plane were hazy, but the pleasure I'd experienced lingered.

I should probably be troubled by the fact that I'd gotten off on being taken while I was half-conscious, but I didn't experience so much as a shadow of shame over what I shared with Massimo. No matter how perverted his games could become, nothing had ever felt more natural than being safe in his masterful hands.

"We're home," Massimo announced when the car stopped in front of a gorgeous, pale yellow building with white balconies. Luxury shops lined the street on the ground floor, but the five stories above were obviously apartments. Pedestrians strolled along the sidewalk, skirting around diners seated at an outdoor café on the corner.

I'd dreamed of visiting Italy for years, and this neighborhood was exactly as I'd imagined it.

Home. I would live here with Massimo. This was my life now, my future. And I would share it with him.

It seemed too wonderful to be real, so much more beautiful and romantic than the mundane future I'd imagined back in Albuquerque when I'd been engaged to George. That life had been one of duty and desperation to please a man who would never be satisfied with me.

Massimo promised me affection, stability, and the opportunity to explore my art. Already, my fingers itched for the camera he'd gifted me, eager to capture images of my new home.

He opened the door of the SUV and helped me step out onto the sidewalk in front of the beautiful yellow building. His strong arm closed around my waist, and he guided me to the intricately carved wooden double doors. He waved a key fob in front of a security pad, and a lock disengaged. He entered with a smooth turn of the large brass knob that decorated the door, welcoming me inside with him.

We crossed a cavernous foyer to a black cage elevator that looked old enough to give me pause. He urged me toward it.

"It's perfectly safe, and we're on the top floor. I don't want you taking the stairs yet."

I complied without protest, even though I felt fit enough for the stairs. I'd barely moved for long weeks, so I should work out to build my strength and stamina. It was a hot, sunny day, and although the foyer was cooler than outside, I would probably work up a sweat by the time I climbed to the top floor.

Despite its aged appearance, the elevator glided upward without rattling, and I breathed a small sigh of relief. His arm firmed around me in reassurance, and I rested my head on his shoulder as we ascended.

When we reached the top floor, he unlocked the apartment door, picked me up, and carried me over the threshold. A delighted giggle burst from my chest as he spun me in a circle, giving me a dizzying first look at the opulent space we would share.

Cream colored walls with intricate crown molding were decorated with abstract paintings in bold, bright pops of color. We were in a short entrance hall, but he quickly walked deeper into the apartment, eager to show me more.

Sunlight peeked through heavy, rich yellow drapes that covered the enormous windows that lined one side of the living room. A glimpse through a doorway on our left showed a hint of a thoroughly modern kitchen, and to my right, I noted a large dining room. All of the furniture appeared to be a blend of cushy comfort but with antique accents: dark carved wood and cream damask upholstery.

He set me down on my feet, but he didn't break contact, taking my hand in his to lead me toward one of the massive windows.

He pulled the drapes back, revealing a glass door that opened out onto a small balcony with a white-painted wooden rail. Delicate garden furniture crafted in wrought iron provided intimate seating and a small dining table.

My breath caught at the stunning view out to the azure sea. The harbor was dotted with sailboats and a handful of yachts, bright spots of white on the gently rolling waves. The coastline curved, showcasing pastel buildings that trailed off into the distance. Miles away, Mount Vesuvius dominated the skyline, deep blue peaks a few shades darker than the sea at the horizon.

Massimo's big hands bracketed my waist from behind, and his lips teased the shell of my ear. "Do you like it?"

I turned to him, my eyes stinging with the depth of my emotion. "It's perfect." My voice wavered slightly. "More beautiful than anything I could've ever imagined."

I looked deep into his shining silver eyes as I spoke, my words encompassing so much more than the stunning scenery and opulent apartment.

He caressed my cheek. "You deserve so much more, *farfallina*. It's only one bedroom, so we will buy somewhere bigger soon. I'll show you around Naples, and we'll find the perfect home for us. This should be comfortable enough for now."

"I love it," I said with the weight of a promise. "I'm so happy to be here with you, Massimo." My throat tightened, squeezing the words I wasn't sure I was ready to say.

I loved this beautiful, damaged, dangerous man.

Before I could muster up the courage to declare

my feelings, a doorbell rang, breaking the intimate moment.

Massimo dropped a kiss on my forehead and went inside to meet his guest. I trailed after him, slight anxiety nipping at me. I didn't know anyone in Naples, and Massimo's friends would likely be associated with the Camorra.

I took a quick breath and reminded myself of all the times he'd protected me, putting his own life on the line. He would never introduce me to someone who might pose a threat.

He opened the apartment door, and two men stepped into the living room. I recognized them as Massimo's friends who had been in Mexico City when I'd first met him. They'd been in Duarte's building on the night I'd run away from George and *Los Zetas.*

Massimo returned to me and took my hand, giving it a gentle squeeze in a pulse of support.

"Evelyn, these are my friends, Gian and Enzo Franco."

He gestured at the men in turn, indicating that Gian was the one with the military-short haircut and shrewd light in his dark green eyes. Enzo's eyes were the exact same shade, but his square jaw was stubble-shaded, and his dark hair fell around his chiseled features to frame his harshly masculine face. A hint of a scar was visible at his right cheekbone, but it did nothing to diminish his ruggedly attractive demeanor. The two men were identically broad and tall, but not quite as big as Massimo. They were dressed in sharply tailored pants and button-down shirts. Enzo was in all black with his sleeves rolled up casually, a contrast to Gian's crisp white shirt and rigid bearing.

Gian nodded at me. "It's good to meet you properly. Massimo has been hiding you away from us." His voice was warm and charming despite his harsh appearance. He offered me a dazzling grin, and it almost reached his keen eyes.

He was assessing me, passing judgment. I lifted my chin and met his sharp stare with a bland smile of my own.

"Massimo has been taking care of me in Mexico City," I corrected him. "But I'm very happy to be here with him now."

Enzo didn't bother with charm. He cocked his head at me, his assessment more blatant than his brother's.

Massimo lifted my hand and brushed a kiss over my knuckles. "It's good to be home."

Warmth suffused my cheeks, my body just as

responsive to his touch as it had been on the night we'd first met.

"Can I get you a drink?" he asked his friends. "I was about to open a bottle of Champagne."

Gian shook his head. "We need to meet with the boss. He wants to talk to you about our new friendship with Duarte and Rodríguez. You've been gone longer than we anticipated."

He'd been delayed in his return because I'd been shot, and he'd chosen to stay in Mexico until I was fully recovered.

"I want to get Evelyn settled," Massimo said, his thumb caressing my palm.

"I'm afraid this can't wait," Gian countered. "You know Salerno isn't a patient man."

"I'll stay here with Evelyn," Enzo offered, his face still impassive. "We can get acquainted."

Anxiety fluttered in my belly, but I smiled up at Massimo, reassuring him. "Go on. I'll be fine here."

"I wanted to show you around the neighborhood," he said, his tone low with regret.

"There will be plenty of time for that later," I said firmly. I didn't want him getting into trouble with his boss because of me. He'd already given me so much. I could overcome my nervousness and spend time with his friend while he saw to his business.

I went up onto my toes and kissed him, a quick but fierce goodbye. "I'll be right here, waiting for you to come home."

His eyes sparked with pale blue fire, an all-consuming hunger that was mirrored in my own soul.

"I'll make it up to you later. I promise."

Massimo always kept his promises. I pressed one final kiss to his lips and urged him to go with Gian.

They left together, and a beat of awkward silence passed between Enzo and me.

"Would you like some of that Champagne Massimo mentioned?" he asked.

"No, thank you." I didn't need to get tipsy; I wanted to keep my wits about me so that I could navigate a conversation with a clearly dangerous man.

I'd grown accustomed to Massimo's aura of danger, but I'd never been fully at ease around his criminal associates. I'd never gotten used to Stefano Duarte's fearsome, mercurial demeanor. Enzo didn't seem maniacal like the Mexican drug lord, but he was a stranger to me. I would be a fool to let my guard down.

He brushed past me, walking into the kitchen as though he was in his own home. "Let's see what's in the fridge."

I followed him, taking in the modern, high-end appliances and marble topped kitchen island while keeping most of my focus on him.

"San Pellegrino?" he suggested as he surveyed the contents of the refrigerator.

"That sounds great. Thanks."

It was a bit bizarre and slightly surreal that a mafioso was offering me a drink in the apartment that was now my own home. I felt off balance and out of place without Massimo's reassuring presence, but I squared my shoulders, determined to navigate this strange, unfamiliar situation.

He passed me a frosted can of lemon San Pellegrino and kept a second one for himself.

"Why don't we sit out on the balcony?" I offered, deciding to play the part of hostess. This was my home, and he was my guest. He was one of Massimo's closest friends, so that meant he would be my friend too.

We settled into the surprisingly comfortable cushioned chairs on the balcony and sat in silence for a minute. Some of my anxious tension melted as I took in the stunning view once again, marveling that this would be my life now. I longed for my camera, but it was still packed away with my clothes. Unable to resist, I lifted my new phone and snapped a shot of the beautiful vista.

"The lifestyle the Camorra affords must be worth it," Enzo drawled, dragging my attention back to him. His forest green eyes were keen on my face, his head canted to the side as he studied me.

"What do you mean?" Some of my tension gripped my chest again at the mention of his criminal organization, but I would become accustomed to it. For Massimo, I would accept this darker aspect of his life.

Enzo gestured around us, encompassing the lavish apartment and the sea view. "All of this is yours now. Beats a DEA agent's meager salary."

I sat up straighter, my spine stiffening at the mention of George. I didn't like his implication.

"I'm not with Massimo for his money." I managed to keep my voice cool and firm, hiding my spike of indignation.

He directed a pointed glance at my neck. "Those diamonds say otherwise."

I met his challenging stare head-on. "I tried to refuse the diamonds and the fancy clothes. The expense made me uncomfortable, but these things make Massimo happy. That's what matters to me. He told me that he grew up with nothing, and he's sacrificed so much in order to survive. His money makes him feel secure after years of deprivation. If seeing that wealth reflected on me gives him satisfaction, I won't deny him."

Enzo rested a corded forearm on the small table, leaning toward me as his gaze sharpened to something even more incisive. "I doubt the money made it difficult for you to leave your fiancé behind."

I crossed my arms over my chest, irritation and defensiveness getting the better of me. "You don't know anything about my relationship with George. Massimo saved me from him, and I will always be grateful for that."

"You mean he saved you from *Los Zetas*." Enzo tried to correct me. "My best friend jumped in front of a bullet for you. How do I know you won't discard him as easily as you left your fiancé?"

My cheeks heated with righteous anger. "I meant exactly what I said: Massimo saved me from George. I will never leave him."

Enzo's eyes darkened, and his mouth thinned to a harsh slash, as though he'd bitten into something sour. "Crawford abused you."

It wasn't a question.

Judging by his thunderous expression, Enzo didn't like it any more than Massimo did. It seemed they shared similar moral compasses; neither of them approved of innocent people being hurt.

It shouldn't surprise me, given their shared history and the way Massimo talked about his friends, as though they were his own brothers. My dark savior would never have such a strong bond with cruel, callous men.

I softened toward Enzo, uncrossing my arms and leaning toward him so that he could read my sincerity plainly on my face.

"I will never do anything to hurt Massimo," I vowed.

I love him. I barely held the words in. I hadn't said them to Massimo yet, and it didn't feel right to tell his friend first.

"I appreciate that you feel protective of him," I continued, "but so do I. He's risked his life for me. I would do anything for him."

Enzo nodded. "He told me that you were shot."

"You're giving me too much credit," I replied. "I was collateral damage when Duarte's cartel was attacked. I couldn't get to Massimo before I was shot."

"But you're choosing to be with him despite

what happened to you. And it's not about his money."

I lifted my chin. "I won't leave him. I don't think I'm capable of it."

I gave him raw honesty. Massimo's friend had to understand that I truly wanted to share my life with my dark protector, and that meant Enzo's opinion mattered to me.

He lifted his drink, tipping it in my direction in a small toast. "Welcome to the family, Evelyn."

My chest warmed at his acceptance. He'd interrogated me to make sure my intentions were pure. I'd never trusted in a friend who had my back like that. Maybe one day, I would earn Enzo's friendship too.

"*Grazie*," I replied in Italian.

A small smile played around his mouth. "Do you speak Italian?"

"I'm learning," I admitted. "It would help if I practice."

"Then we'll practice," he encouraged. "Tell me what you want to see most now that you're in Naples."

I switched into Italian, haltingly telling him how I'd always wanted to visit the Amalfi Coast and Capri. I shared my passion for photography and how Massimo had sweetly gifted me with a camera. He believed in my art, and I wanted Enzo to know how much that meant to me.

As we spoke, his handsome features lit up in a bright grin, transforming from the forbidding mask into an expression of genuine approval.

My heart soared with hope for my happy future.

Chapter 7

Massimo

Violent tension instantly gripped my muscles when Gian and I stepped into Salerno's study. It wasn't hatred of our sadistic boss that put me on edge; it was the man who was seated in one of the black leather armchairs as though he belonged there.

Rocco Abate leered at me, a vicious baring of teeth rather than a true smile. The expression twisted his scarred features, the ruined left side of his face puckering into a nightmarish mask.

I barely suppressed a snarl of soul-deep hatred as I stared down the man who'd killed my parents. The sight of his horrific face didn't quell my murderous loathing—I'd inflicted that damage with the broken bottle I'd used to defend my family all those years ago. His blood had dripped from the jagged glass as I watched the light leave my mother's eyes.

"What is he doing here?" I demanded of Salerno, the question little more than a growl.

Rocco was a member of the Nardone clan, our rivals who controlled the territory to the north of our own turf. We'd established a tenuous truce over the years, neither clan willing to incite a war. That would be bad for business.

But now that my friends and I had forged an alliance with Duarte and Rodríguez, we would be powerful enough to take on this motherfucker. Gian would overthrow Salerno in his long-awaited coup, and then I would be free to finally exact my revenge on Rocco. Gian would support me in the violence against the Nardone clan, but it would be over quickly now that we were responsible for the lucrative new trafficking route into Europe.

Gian had aspirations that extended beyond Naples, even past the Italian border. Soon, he planned to reach out to our Irish and Dutch counterparts. More alliances would be formed, and power would be consolidated. We would be kings, and the piece of shit who'd murdered my parents would be in the ground.

"Rocco has a proposition for us," Salerno

drawled, a small smile ghosting around his thin lips; cruel pleasure at my expense. The sadistic bastard relished the fact that I barely harnessed my rage out of deference to him.

Gian placed a restraining hand on my shoulder, a firm reminder of all that was at stake if I defied Salerno and attacked Rocco now.

Soon. I would kill him as soon as Gian came to power. My fingers already itched with the need to wrap around his throat.

"He wants in on our new deal with the cartels," Salerno continued. "He's willing to kill his boss and pledge his loyalty to me. The Nardone clan's territory will be ours, and Rocco will be rewarded for his part in our victory."

Gian didn't bother to hide his disdain, his upper lip curling in a sneer. "Any man who would betray his brothers isn't trustworthy. We should send him back to his boss and force him to confess his traitorous plan. Massimo can make sure to leave his tongue intact so that he can tell his clan exactly what he tried to do."

I wasn't certain if I was capable of the restraint required to make him bleed without taking his life. But the prospect of hearing my enemy's screams elevated my pulse, adrenaline flooding my system in anticipation of the violence.

"And what about you, Massimo?" Rocco challenged, his beady eyes glinting with delight. "I heard a rumor that your new woman was fucking a DEA agent back in America. Is she trustworthy? Are you? Or are you letting your dick rule your decisions?"

Gian's fingers bit into my shoulder, barely restraining me. Red clouded the edges of my vision, and my body practically vibrated with the need to kill. He knew about Evelyn. He was trying to turn Salerno against her, so that my boss would target her as a potential threat.

"Anyone who touches Evelyn will die screaming." I kept my glower on Rocco but included Salerno in the threat.

"Surely, you're not going to allow this son of a bitch to come into your home and threaten us," Gian demanded of Salerno. His tone was cool and calm, but the words were a challenge. "Send him back to his boss in pieces. He can still breathe without his limbs intact."

"I want the Nardone territory," our boss replied coldly. "Rocco will deliver."

Gian lifted his chin. "We don't need this traitor to take their territory. We have the connections to cut off their business now. They won't be able to compete with us for much longer. They'll be broke within a year, and they'll turn on each other."

Salerno cocked his head at my friend, his dark eyes calculating. After a long, tense minute, he nodded.

"I won't make our people bleed to eliminate the Nardone clan. If you can guarantee their downfall within a year, that's the prudent move. But I would prefer that they don't know what we're planning." His glacial gaze fixed on Rocco. "You won't breathe a word about this meeting to your boss, and I will allow you to leave here in one piece."

"No," I snarled, taking a step toward my enemy. "He's mine."

I couldn't let him walk out of here. Not when he'd made it clear that his attention was on Evelyn.

"If we kill him, his boss will think we're going to war," Gian told me quietly. "Not yet, Massimo."

Rocco got to his feet and spared a shrug in Salerno's direction. "Your loss."

Salerno scowled at him, his grim expression promising a slow death. "I'll let Massimo have you when the time comes."

My blood burned in my veins, a toxic mix of resentment and vicious anticipation. Rocco would die by my hand, but not at Salerno's command. The cruel old bastard wouldn't control me for much longer.

I sucked in a breath and leashed my darkest impulses. Allowing my most hated enemy to stroll away unscathed took every shred of my willpower.

Chapter 8

Evelyn

"Evelyn!" Massimo thundered my name as he burst into the apartment, breaking up my pleasant conversation with Enzo.

My heart leapt into my throat, and I raced inside from the balcony to find out what was wrong; he sounded half-panicked.

His eyes glinted with a wild light, and his massive body was taut with strain. He closed the distance between us in three long strides and scooped me up into his powerful arms.

"I'll see you both later." Enzo excused himself, giving us privacy to discuss whatever had upset my dark savior.

"Are you okay?" I asked as he carried me into the bedroom—*our* bedroom.

I only had a moment to get a brief impression of the sumptuous, deep blue room before he laid me out on the four-poster bed and settled his hulking body over mine, as though he was shielding me from something.

His jaw was tight, but his thick fingers were achingly gentle as they trailed through my hair. The motion was meant to soothe me, but I sensed that it calmed him too.

I traced the harsh lines of his beautiful face. "Talk to me. What happened?"

He closed his eyes briefly and blew out a long breath. "I'm all right," he promised. "And you're all right. That's what matters."

"Of course I'm all right," I reassured him. "I've just been safely at home, chatting with Enzo. Did something bad happen at your meeting?"

He shook his head slightly. "I don't want to talk to you about my business, *dolcezza*. I think we will both prefer it that way."

I kissed his taut jaw. "I want to talk about *you*. I care about how you're feeling. You don't have to tell me anything else."

I'd made my peace with his criminal lifestyle when I'd chosen to come to Italy with him. We would find a balance that worked for us. His happiness mattered more to me than anything, and I didn't want him to ever hide his emotions from me.

"I didn't like being separated from you," he admitted. "Something happened that made me worried for your safety, but I swear, I'll never let anyone touch you. This is my home, and I'm powerful enough to protect you."

I brushed a stray curl that fell over his eyes. "It's *our* home now," I reminded him. "And I know you'll protect me. I trust you, Massimo."

He crushed his lips to mine and claimed me with savagery that bordered on desperation. I softened in his arms, welcoming his harsh claim.

His hands fisted in my soft cotton dress, tearing at the lightweight material in his frenzy to strip me bare for him. His feverish intensity swept me up too, and I fumbled at the buttons on his crisp white shirt. He jerked it off, the last two buttons popping free and pinging across the hardwood floor.

I reached for his belt, but he pulled back, kissing his way down my sternum and bare belly. He caught my pink lace panties between his teeth, and the delicate underwear tore away. A rush of heat wet my lower lips, my body primed for him.

He licked me with one long swipe of his tongue,

ending with a flick over my clit. Stars burst across my vision, and I arched into him with a sharp cry. His fingers sank into my thighs, pinning me exactly where he wanted me. He began to feast on my pussy like he'd been starving for me, relentlessly toying with my clit. Ecstasy crashed through me in a sudden shockwave, and he growled against me as he tasted my orgasm.

I began to squirm away from the overwhelming rush of sensation on my sensitive bud, but he pressed his palm down on my stomach, trapping me. My fingers twined in his dark curls, and I wasn't sure if I was trying to push him away or pull him closer for more erotic torment.

Two thick fingers eased inside me, expertly finding my g-spot and forcing another orgasm from my taut body. My legs shook, so I wrapped them around his shoulders to steady myself. He anchored me to reality, my rock in the storm of ruthless pleasure.

He withdrew his fingers from my tight channel, tracing the line of my swollen folds before exploring farther back. I jolted when he brushed over my asshole.

"Massimo!" His name was half-protest, half-plea. Forbidden pleasure crackled through me at the light stimulation. No one had ever touched me there before. It was wrong, perverse.

"This tight little hole belongs to me," he growled, the possessive words vibrating over my pulsing clit. "Your beautiful body is all mine. One day, I'll fuck your gorgeous ass. I'll make sure you're ready for me."

"I can't," I panted, my entire body heating with embarrassment and dark desire. "Massimo, please..."

"You can," he commanded, sliding one desire slicked finger past my tight ring of muscles. "You will. You will give me everything, Evelyn. All of you. I own you."

I clamped down on his invading finger, struggling to resist the penetration. My cheeks flamed, and my thighs quaked. He licked the fresh wash of my wanton desire from my throbbing sex and hummed his approval.

"Good girl. You love being mine, don't you? You'll do anything for me."

The last wasn't a question; it was the absolute truth. I would give this man anything he asked of me. And I trusted him to make me feel good. He brought me transcendent ecstasy, and there was no room for shame or shyness between us. I trusted him completely.

I took a breath and relaxed, allowing his finger to slide deeper.

"That's it," he encouraged. "You're being so good for me, *farfallina*. Such a brave girl."

His praise was a trigger, and my orgasm crested before his tongue touched my pussy again. The rush of bliss elicited by his approval sent me flying high, and my inner muscles contracted with only his finger stimulating me.

His teeth grazed my clit, and I screamed his name, my back bowing with the force of my orgasm.

When I was trembling and utterly spent, he pressed one final kiss to my inner thigh and pulled away. He towered over me, his eyes shining like a predatory wolf who'd just cornered his prey. I stared up at him, panting and slightly dizzy from the relentless pleasure he'd wrung from my helpless body. His sensual lips curved in a wicked smirk, a dark expression of masculine arrogance and satisfaction.

He grasped my hips and abruptly flipped me over. One strong arm hooked around me, pulling me up onto my knees while his other hand applied pressure to my shoulders. He positioned me so that my back arched, my ass offered up to him. His long fingers encircled my neck from behind, pressing my cheek into the pillow. The dominant squeeze on my nape made me soften instinctively, and I submitted to his will with a long, contented sigh. I let go of all my worries and insecurities. An invisible weight lifted from me, and I felt light enough to float away. Only his hand on my neck kept me tethered to reality, and my full focus centered on him.

"Stay," he commanded.

A sharp, shocking slap resounded through the bedroom, and stinging heat bloomed on my bottom. He'd spanked me to reinforce his order. It hadn't been necessary to earn my submission, but the dominant act made me sink deeper into the power he held over me. The strength of his will supported me, his control setting me free. The heat from the spanking sank deeper into my flesh, reaching my aching core. I'd already lost track of my orgasms, but I needed him inside me, needed to feel him filling me up until he branded me with his cum.

I heard a drawer opening, but I kept my face meekly pressed against the pillow, remaining exactly where he'd left me. My panting breaths turned deep and even as I fully relaxed into his control.

Something cold and slick dropped onto my exposed asshole, and I yelped in shock. His arm around my waist anchored me in place, reassuring me even as he trapped me.

"I'm going to plug your ass," he told me. "We'll start training you so that you can take my cock one day."

He petted my bottom, his fingers trailing lightly over the spot where he'd spanked me. My sensitive skin tingled, and a light shiver raced through me.

"That's it," he encouraged. "Relax, and trust me."

I nodded. I trusted him with my life, my heart, my soul.

"I'm yours," I murmured, the promise breathy with lustful devotion.

The tip of the plug pressed against my tight hole. I took a deep breath and released all of my lingering tension on a long exhale, allowing him to penetrate me with the toy. He gently pumped it into me, the slow thrusts lighting up sensitive pleasure centers I hadn't known I possessed.

My breaths came quicker, elevated with desire and a hint of strain as I struggled to accept the strange intrusion. He shushed me gently and toyed with my clit with his free hand. Pleasure washed through me in a warm wave, and the plug slid deeper inside me.

A light burning sensation edged into my pleasure, and I turned my face into the pillow with a soft whine.

"You can take it," he promised. "You're being such a good girl for me. Almost there."

The widest part of the plug slipped into me, and my tight ring of muscles closed around the narrower base. I felt almost unbearably full, stretched in a way that was utterly foreign and slightly uncomfortable. He continued toying with my clit, and the discomfort morphed into dark pleasure.

"Are you ready for me, *dolcezza*?"

He stroked my aching folds, and my core clenched.

"Yes," I whispered, feeling small and vulnerable. "I need you, Massimo."

"You have me, Evelyn. All of me."

He dropped a sweet kiss on my heated cheek and then quickly finished stripping, baring his stunning body. I watched him hungrily as he undressed for me, taking in his muscular arms, the way his abs rippled. His powerful thighs flexed as he climbed onto the bed with me, positioning himself behind me. I struggled to keep him in my line of sight, but he soothed me with a long stroke of his calloused palm down my spine.

He tapped on the base of the plug, and I released

a sharp cry at the ripples of pleasure that pulsed through me.

His low laugh rumbled through me, his arrogant pleasure intoxicating. He'd laid claim to every inch of my body, and I was still greedy for more.

"Please..." I begged, lifting my ass in offering.

"I do love when you beg," he rumbled. "How can I deny you?"

His hard cock lined up with my slick opening, and he penetrated me in a slow slide. I gasped, and my fingers tangled in the sheets, gripping them as though I clung to the bed. The rush of dark ecstasy was almost vicious, clawing through me and shredding my thoughts until I was reduced to a purely primal state.

I moaned and rocked back against him, and he cursed as he entered me to the hilt. He gripped my hips, his fingers flexing into my soft flesh as he held us both still. His cock jerked inside me, and he released an animal growl of his own, clinging to his control.

"You're so tight," he hissed, running a reverent hand down my back. "So perfect. And all mine."

I groaned my agreement, beyond words. He slowly pulled back, his cockhead dragging over my g-spot. A high, keening sound caught in my throat, and I grasped at the sheets.

He thrust back inside me, his hips pressing the plug deeper into my ass. I released a guttural shout and writhed as relentless ecstasy coursed through me. His fingers bit into my hips, and he started fucking me, hard and fast. With each feral thrust, he sent me flying higher. I wasn't sure when my orgasm started, but it continued to build, ripping through my body with merciless force. Blissful tears wet my cheek, and he leaned over me to kiss them, tasting the flavor of my complete subjugation.

My utter surrender triggered his release, and he came undone on a primal snarl. He pumped into me, forcing the last ripples of helpless pleasure from my pulsing sex. His hot seed lashed me, marking me as his.

As he gently pulled out of me and cradled my spent body, he stroked my sweat-slicked skin. Low words of praise rumbled over me in a steady stream of Italian. I'd started to learn the language, but I didn't take the time to puzzle out the meaning. I closed my eyes and drifted, basking in the complete perfection of being owned by Massimo.

Chapter 9

Evelyn

The sun shone on Massimo's golden skin, his muscular chest on full display. My body heated for him, and I was grateful for the cool breeze created by the forward motion of the speedboat. He wrapped one arm around me and steered the boat with his other hand. I leaned into him in complete contentment. To our right, the island of Capri rose from the sea, ancient rock jutting up from the water. The lush greenery was dotted with pale pastel villas and clusters of shops.

As we rounded the small island, the iconic Faraglioni formation appeared before us: three massive, pale grey rocks emerging from the azure sea. Massimo slowed the boat so that we cruised peacefully toward the arch in the center of one of the rocks. It looked small from this distance, but as we neared the massive landmarks, I realized that the arch formed a large enough passage for our boat to glide through it.

I lifted my camera and captured the imposing sight, taking a dozen shots of the scenery before my focus was drawn inexorably back to my dark savior. His low chuckle rumbled over me as he placed a hand on top of my camera, gently urging me to lower it.

"You can't photograph me all the time," he chided. "No one will want to buy those pictures."

I defied him with a sly smile, lifting my Canon again to capture his sun kissed face and flashing eyes. Their pale, silvery blue mirrored the sea, like the glittering sunlight that danced on the water.

"Who says I'm selling my art? What if I'm selfish enough to keep these images for myself?"

He laughed again, and the rich sound rolled through me in a wave of warm happiness. "All right, *farfallina*. You can keep the pictures of me for your own private use." He tucked a stray lock of blonde hair behind my ear, and I blushed at his implication. "But don't you want to share your art with the world?"

My heart lifted at the thought. "I don't know if

I'm good enough," I admitted. "I've always dreamed of having my photographs in a gallery somewhere, but that will take years of work building a reputation for myself."

He curled two fingers beneath my chin, lifting my face to his. "I believe in you, Evelyn. You can do anything you want to do. You are talented enough, and you deserve success. The world needs more beauty in it. You have so much to offer."

"And what do you want?" I pressed, wishing him equal happiness to what he was promising me.

"You," he replied, the single word resonating through my soul.

I flushed with pleasure but pushed a bit more, "What do you want for your future? You have me already."

He took a moment to consider his answer. "I want security for us both. I want to provide a home for you and build a life that we can share. Soon, we'll be totally free to make our own choices."

"You don't feel free now?"

He cupped my nape, his thick fingers sliding into my hair. "I've never been totally free to pursue the future I want. I've fought for every scrap of freedom I have. I want to choose my own path. That's what I'm doing now with Gian and Enzo. We clawed our way out of *Le Vele*, and we paid our dues. I will never be locked up again."

I blinked up at him in surprise. "You were in prison?"

He nodded grimly. "For two years, from sixteen to eighteen."

"What were you arrested for?" I wasn't sure if I wanted to know, but I craved to understand him better.

"I robbed a jewelry store with Enzo. It was mostly cheap shit, but that was how we got by back then. It was how we proved ourselves." He shrugged as though it didn't bother him, but I noted the tension around his eyes. "Everyone gets locked up sooner or later. I don't intend to repeat the experience." He kissed my furrowed brow. "Don't worry, *dolcezza*. I'm untouchable now. I won't ever leave you, and I'll never be under someone else's control ever again."

My heart ached for him, for the desperate circumstances that'd shaped him. I understood his need to dominate me now. He'd never felt fully in control of his life, and controlling my pleasure brought him a sense of satisfaction and peace.

I would gladly give him my body in any way he

desired if it would ease some of his burdens. We would find our freedom together.

He pulled me close and steered the boat toward the arch in the rock. "Kiss me," he murmured against my lips. "It's good luck."

I could hardly believe that I'd been lucky enough to meet this wonderful man, and he was all mine.

I tipped my head back and offered myself to him, pledging my future to him with every caress of my tongue against his. He deepened the kiss as we passed beneath the shadow of the arch, laying claim to everything I promised and making silent vows of his own.

I tried to stop my jaw from hanging open as Massimo led me through the pedestrian streets of Capri; it took effort not to gawk at the beauty of the setting and the luxury items that filled shop windows. He'd already insisted on buying me a new dress, and a pair of large diamond studs now adorned my ears.

We approached an empty shop, and a woman greeted us in front of the glass door.

Massimo introduced himself and me, so it was clear that the woman was a stranger to him. My brow was still pinched with puzzlement when she unlocked the door and gestured for us to enter.

"Call me when you're finished, and I'll lock up whenever you leave," she said warmly. "Take your time. I'll give you some privacy, and I'm happy to accommodate any further requests."

Massimo thanked her, took my hand, and guided me into the empty space.

"What are we doing here?" I asked, confused.

He spread his arms wide to encompass the large, bare space. "Do you like it?"

"The location is beautiful," I replied, uncertain what to say.

He chuckled and pulled me close. "It's for you, *farfallina*. This will be your gallery if you want it."

"What?" I asked on a little puff of air, not sure if I'd heard him correctly.

"I'll buy it for you," he elaborated. "But if you don't like the space, we'll find somewhere else."

I shook my head, my eyes stinging. "It's too much."

He cupped my cheeks in both hands, holding me as though I was his most precious treasure. "Nothing is too much for you."

"But I didn't earn it," I protested. My heart tugged toward his. I wanted to accept, but I couldn't quite shake the lingering sense of unworthiness.

His expression turned stern. "Did you earn your degree?"

"Yes, but I've never sold my art. I've never been featured in a gallery. You can't buy success for me, Massimo."

"I'm not buying your success; that will be your own, and I won't take it from you. But I can provide the space where you can reach others with your art. Whether you succeed or not will be up to you. But I have faith that you will."

"I love you." The words rushed from me in a burst of pure emotion.

His eyes widened with awe for a fraction of a second before he crushed his lips to mine, as though he could taste the promise of my devotion on my tongue.

He stepped toward me, never breaking our kiss as he directed me into the privacy of the back room, away from the large shop window where passersby might see us. He pushed me up against the wall and shoved my dress over my thighs, reaching for my core.

"Tell me again," he commanded, grabbing my sex in a rough, possessive grip.

"I love you," I moaned, rocking my hips into his hand, seeking stimulation.

My clit pulsed with pleasure as he ground his palm against it, his fingers dipping between my slick folds. I was wet and ready for him, desperate to feel him inside me, making love to me. I felt his love in every lash of his tongue against mine and in the harsher graze of his teeth over my lower lip.

"All mine," he growled into my mouth, lavishing me with hungry kisses.

He rotated his hand against my sensitive pussy, and I cried out at the burst of pleasure.

"Your whore is beautiful, but I'd rather see my hands on her."

I yelped at the new, unfamiliar voice. Massimo whirled, placing his massive body between me and the crass stranger.

Five men crowded into the back room with us. They were all armed, and the one at the center of the group—the man who'd spoken—held a gun trained on Massimo's heart.

I cringed at the sight of his scarred face, which was twisted in a maniacal leer.

He jerked his chin in the direction of the back wall, and I noted the open door for the first time. It led into a darkened space, and I glimpsed a concrete wall and stairs.

"We're going into the basement. I wouldn't want anyone to hear your slut screaming."

"You'll be the one screaming," Massimo snarled, his huge body swelling with protective rage. "You're a dead man, Rocco."

Our assailant barked a cruel laugh. "Who's holding the gun here?" he challenged. "I'll shoot you if you reach for your weapon, and then you won't be alive to watch me play with her. That would be a shame. I've been dreaming of the day I get to destroy you for what you did to my face, and you won't rob me of the satisfaction."

"You killed my parents," Massimo growled, and my heart skipped a beat. "I should've ended you that day. You will not touch Evelyn."

Rocco sneered. "I think you'll find that I will touch her as much as I want." He nodded in the direction of the basement again. "Go on. Or I'll make it hurt worse."

Massimo reached for me, taking my hand in a vise grip. "It will be okay, *farfallina*," he promised. "I'll keep you safe."

I wished I could believe him, but even my dark protector couldn't survive a bullet to the heart.

"I'll go with you," I told the monster who'd murdered his parents. "Don't hurt Massimo."

Rocco grinned at me, a horrific baring of teeth. "Watching you scream will hurt him a lot more than shooting him."

My blood ran cold, and I shuddered in revulsion. I looked at the four men who surrounded him, desperately searching for any sign of hesitation or mercy.

I found none. I read my death in their cold eyes, and Rocco's insane leer told me that he would enjoy extracting every second of my suffering.

Chapter 10

Massimo

My heart slammed against my ribcage with bruising force, and fear I'd never known before gripped my lungs with sharp black claws. I struggled to breathe as we descended the stairs into the dank basement, where no one would hear her scream. My enemies had silencers on their guns, so even if I launched myself at them and risked getting shot, no one would be alerted to the fact that we were being attacked in the empty shop.

My own weapon had been taken from me by one of Rocco's goons. I vaguely recognized the four other men as members of his clan.

I kept Evelyn in front of me, and the spot

between my shoulder blades itched where my enemy's gun was still trained on my heart.

"Do your friends know that you tried to betray them?" I asked Rocco, keeping my voice as calm as I could manage. It came out rough and gravelly, but the words were clear enough. Maybe I could convince his friends to turn on him once they learned of his treachery.

His gun slammed into my back, and I barely managed to keep my balance so that I wouldn't knock Evelyn down the stairs.

"They know all about that, you dumb fucker," he taunted. "I came to Salerno to get more information about your deal with the cartels. My boss ordered me to do it. And I was happy to take the opportunity to destroy everything you've worked for. I thought I'd missed my opportunity, but then I saw you with this bitch, and I realized that you're finally vulnerable. Love is weakness, Massimo. I would've thought you learned that the day I killed your pathetic parents."

My mind raced, searching for a way to save her from my worst enemy. I'd shared the app that tracked her movements with Gian and Enzo, just in case I ever needed help finding her. We were supposed to meet them for coffee soon, but I'd lost track of time while I'd been kissing her.

If we didn't show, they might come looking for us. I had no idea how long it might take them to worry over our delay.

Rocco would hurt Evelyn in the meantime. I couldn't bear it. I would tear him apart if he touched so much as a single strand of her platinum hair.

We reached the bottom of the stairs, and I kept my body positioned between the men who threatened us and Evelyn's delicate frame.

Pain cracked through my skull when Rocco smashed his gun into the back of my head. The world flashed with bright light, white lightning filling my vision so that I lost sight of her. I blinked hard and willed the world to stop spinning, but a sharp kick to my gut made my insides writhe. I doubled over on my knees and gasped for air, but my lungs wouldn't expand. Another kick, and my ribs cracked.

Evelyn's screams tore at me, more agonizing than the beating.

The barrage of blows stopped, and I tried to surge to my feet before my balance returned. I dropped back onto one knee, and rough hands grabbed my arms, two men holding me down. In my rage and desperate fear, I would've found the strength to fight them off, but my vision finally cleared to reveal my nightmare.

Rocco clutched Evelyn from behind, using her slight body as a shield. One of his arms wrapped around her waist, pinning her back to his chest. His other hand held a knife to her throat.

My heart twisted, and I went utterly still. One wrong move from me, and he would cut her open. I would watch her bleed out and gasp for air, and there would be nothing I could do to save her.

I'd lost my parents to this monster. My violent impulses had drawn his cruel attention on that awful day, and even though I'd managed to ruin his face, he'd taken something far more precious from me: the only two people in the world who loved me unconditionally.

Now, he held Evelyn's life in his hands. His attention was on her because of her association with me.

"Let her go," I ground out. "She has nothing to do with your vendetta. I'm the one you want to hurt."

Rocco cocked his head at me. "I've seen you with

women before, but never like this. I've been watching you ever since you landed in Naples. You're obsessed with her." He laughed like it was the funniest joke he'd ever heard. "I think you might even love her. It's more than just a good fuck, isn't it?"

Confessing my love now would seal her fate. I was toxic to the people I loved most. She'd told me she loved me, and I hadn't said it back. Because some dark part of me knew this was inevitable: my love for her would kill her.

He licked her pale cheek, and she shuddered in revulsion. Her peridot eyes were wide and wild with terror, and she barely breathed with his blade pressing into her neck. A small bead of blood welled at her throat, and panic clawed me.

"Maybe I should take my turn fucking her before I give her scars to match mine," Rocco mused.

I roared in wordless fury, beyond coherent thought. All I could see was the flash of the knife that could end her life and her pinched, fearful features. A sense of powerlessness hollowed out my chest, and it had nothing to do with the weaker men who had me pinned down. I couldn't so much as flinch without risking her life.

He groped at her chest with his free hand, squeezing her breast hard enough to draw a sharp cry from her.

"I think I want her bleeding when I feel her pussy fighting my cock." He shifted the blade, moving it from her throat to her freckled cheek.

The moment the knife left her neck, I launched myself at him. He might still manage to cut her, but I would have to be faster. I'd always been stronger than my enemy, but I'd never been allowed to challenge him before. Not without risking a war.

Now, I didn't give a fuck about the consequences. My entire being was consumed with the desperate need to wrench her away from him.

I grabbed his wrist, yanking the blade far away from her porcelain skin. With a sharp twist, his bones snapped, and the knife dropped from his limp fingers.

His scream resounded through the cramped basement, immediately accompanied by the muted pops of gunfire. His friends had silencers on their weapons, but none of the bullets hit me.

I shoved Rocco back and put my body between Evelyn and our attackers. As I whirled to face the stairs, I saw Gian and Enzo storming in, their guns drawn. Two of Rocco's goons were already down, bleeding out on the concrete. The firefight was focused on the encroaching threat posed by my friends, and the bullets weren't directed at me.

I trusted the brothers to make quick work of the rest of them.

Rocco wouldn't get such a swift end. He'd killed my parents. He'd terrorized Evelyn. She wouldn't be safe until he was dead.

She mattered far more than any conflict with our rivals. I would go to war for her any day.

I attacked my oldest enemy, rage and years of hatred driving every vicious strike as I methodically broke his body with my bare hands. His bones crunched beneath my fists, and he screamed. I beat him until his face was such a pulverized, bloody mess that he couldn't manage more than a gurgling moan of horror. I wrapped my hands around his throat and squeezed. He thrashed, his limbs too broken to fight me off. His ruined face darkened to a deep shade of purple, and red veins burst across the whites of his eyes.

"He's dead." Gian's voice was low and reassuring, and he touched a tentative hand to my shoulder. As though I was a rabid beast that might turn on him if he spooked me. "Evelyn needs you, Massimo."

Evelyn.

My heart twisted. I'd just gone feral and beaten a man to death right in front of my delicate little butterfly. The last time she'd witnessed such a vicious kill, she'd turned from me in revulsion. She'd been afraid of me.

Fear clutched at my chest again, a budding anxiety that I would see my mother's final look of horror reflected in Evelyn's pale green eyes.

"Massimo." She flung her willowy body against my chest, seeking the comfort of my embrace. Her small hands roved over me, searching for injuries. "They hurt you."

"I'm all right, *dolcezza*," I promised, my knees going weak at the rush of relief that swept through my system.

Her arms around me gave me the strength I needed to remain standing. My head and my ribs ached, but I wasn't seriously injured.

I pulled back slightly so that I could peer down into her lovely eyes. They were still wide with fear. My stomach turned.

"Don't be afraid, *farfallina*." I practically begged her not to fear me.

She caressed my tight jaw. "I'm not afraid of you. I'm afraid *for* you. They beat you. We have to get you to a doctor."

"It's nothing serious, but I'll call my physician. We can meet him at our home, and he'll check me over. I'm sure it's just some bruising."

I touched my fingers beneath her chin, turning her face so that I could inspect her. Not even a scratch marred her perfect complexion. I'd managed to wrench Rocco's knife away before he cut her. The tiny bead of crimson at her throat remained, but the cut was so shallow that the bleeding had already stopped.

My sweet girl had been tormented, but she was concerned for me. I knew her well enough to realize that she wouldn't be soothed until the doctor confirmed that I was okay.

"Let's go home." I picked her up and cradled her to my chest. "Close your eyes. I've got you."

I didn't want her to have to look at the dead bodies that littered the basement.

"We'll clean up here," Enzo promised.

I nodded my thanks, and Evelyn obediently closed her eyes, tucking her face against my shoulder.

The brothers would ensure that no one knew five men had been killed in this basement.

"And I'll handle the Nardone clan," Enzo added. "There won't be a war. I'll make sure of it."

I didn't linger to ask about his plans. If he had a

way to avoid a conflict, I trusted him to handle it. Evelyn was my only concern now.

The woman I loved had been terrorized by my worst enemy, but he was finally dead. He would never touch her again. He would never hurt my family.

Chapter 11

Evelyn

"Talk to me, *farfallina*," Massimo urged, cuddling me against him in our bed.

"I'm okay," I promised, crushing my residual fear and horror into a tight ball and shoving it deep into my chest. "The doctor said I'm fine. Barely a scratch on me. You're the one with bruised ribs."

He frowned down at me. "Don't do that with me."

I blinked at him. "Do what?"

"Lie to us both. You don't have to pretend to be okay. I don't want you to hide your feelings in an attempt to spare me from worry. I want to know all of your emotions, even the darker ones. Nothing you say will make me abandon you."

My throat tightened. How could he see me so clearly? He peered straight into my soul, understanding me in a way I hardly even knew myself.

For years, I'd hidden my more distressing emotions. I'd made myself small because I didn't want to be difficult. I was afraid people would rebuke me for it like my mother, or worse, that they would abandon me like my father. George had never noticed how I concealed my darker emotions from him to make his life easier. Or maybe he had noticed, but he'd allowed me to diminish myself.

"You can be vulnerable with me," Massimo cajoled. "I want you to be yourself when we're together, even if that means talking about difficult things. You don't have to shoulder those burdens on your own anymore. Trust me to share them with you."

My heart swelled with love for him, and I snuggled closer to his hard chest, breathing him in.

"I was so scared," I admitted on a shaky whisper. "I thought they were going to kill you."

He stroked my hair. "I was scared too. I've never felt fear like that. Rocco hurt you, and I had to watch." His features hardened to granite. "It will never happen again."

A light shiver raced through me before I could stop it.

No, it wouldn't happen again. Because the man who'd killed his parents, Rocco, was dead. Massimo had beaten and strangled him. I'd squeezed my eyes shut tight for most of it, but I'd seen enough of the violence to disturb me.

"I'm sorry you saw that," he rumbled, his voice rough with regret.

I brushed a reassuring kiss over his taut lips. "You protected me. You saved us both. I will never like the violence, Massimo, but I understand. I'm not afraid of you."

He blew out a shaky breath. "If I could make sure that you will never feel fear again, I would. But I swear I will do everything in my power to prevent it."

"I know. I trust you." I kissed him again, then asked, "How are you feeling? That man, Rocco, he killed your parents, didn't he? You must've hated him for a long time."

His eyes searched mine, and he was silent for a long moment. I wasn't sure if he was puzzling through his own complicated feelings or if he was trying to put them into words that wouldn't upset me. I met his gaze with an open heart, waiting for him to speak his truth. I would accept anything he said, even if it might be disturbing. I accepted all of him, and I would prove it to him every day, just as he'd proven himself to me so many times.

"Yes," he finally said quietly. "I hated him. I still do. I'm not sure if that hatred will ever fade, but at least I have the peace of knowing he'll never hurt anyone else. Their deaths have been avenged." He shook his head. "But I don't feel any different. They're still gone. And it will always be my fault."

I trailed my fingers through his dark curls, careful not to press the tender spot where he'd been hit. He leaned into my touch and closed his eyes briefly, as though he was savoring the tender contact.

"Rocco took them from you," I said gently. "He's responsible. You were just a boy in a difficult situation. You have to forgive yourself."

His eyes flashed with silver fire. "I don't know if I can."

He'd carried the weight of responsibility for their deaths for so many years that he didn't know how to live without it.

I pressed a gentle kiss to his furrowed brow. "You are forgiven."

It wasn't in my power to forgive him, but if he

heard the words spoken aloud, he might one day say them to himself.

"You protected me today," I reassured him. "You made sure that he can't hurt me again. He will never take anyone else's family away from them. You did what was right. You're a good man, Massimo."

His eyes were tight with something like longing. He wanted to believe me.

"I love you," I vowed. "Nothing will change that."

His lips met mine in an achingly gentle caress. There was quiet desperation in the kiss, a slight tension lingering around his mouth. I trailed my fingertips along his stubble-roughened jaw, soothing him as I opened for him on a sigh. I welcomed him to claim me with soft flicks of my tongue against his. He groaned, almost a sound of pain, and surrendered to our chemistry.

He grasped my hips and rolled onto his back, pulling me upright so that I straddled him. His deft fingers found the delicate zipper at the back of my dress, and he made quick work of stripping me down to my underwear.

When he jerked his own shirt over his head, I pulled back. A dark bruise marred his left side where his enemies had viciously kicked him.

"I don't want to hurt you," I murmured, lightly touching my palm to his heart.

"The only thing you can do that will hurt me is to deny me," he rasped, his flame blue eyes burning into my soul. "I love you, Evelyn."

My heart skipped a beat, and my breath caught. I'd declared my feelings for him, but I hadn't been prepared for the overwhelming surge of emotion that was elicited by those sweet words dropping from his beautiful lips. Because looking into his shining eyes, I could see into his soul too. The love he offered me was fierce and unconditional. I would never have to prove myself to him. I would never have to earn his affection and approval.

I was enough for him, just as I was.

And he was more than enough for me; he was better than anything I'd ever dared to dream for myself.

Words stuck in my constricted throat, so I worshipped his body with my mouth, dropping hungry, reverent kisses on his jaw, his throat, his chest. I traced the shape of his abs with my tongue, and they rippled beneath me as his hand sank into my hair. He didn't guide me lower or demand anything of me, but his firm grip anchored me to him.

I unbuckled his belt and quickly freed his cock so that I could taste him. His hard length jutted toward me, and I didn't hesitate to take him into my mouth. I wrapped my lips around him and welcomed him in one slow slide, suppressing my gag reflex so that I could accommodate all of his impressive length.

He murmured my name like a prayer, and his fingers tightened in my hair, holding me down on his shaft. I softened and stayed where he wanted me, allowing him to control my breath. He had all of me. I gave myself to him willingly, eagerly.

When I began to feel dizzy, he tugged me off of him. My lips grasped at his cockhead, and my tongue swirled around him in regret as he pulled his cock free.

"I want you," I begged in a breathy whisper.

"You have me, *dolcezza*. But I'm not finished with you yet. I won't be for a long time."

He settled his body over mine and eased into me, his cock stretching me inch by delicious inch. He kissed me long and deep, his tongue thrusting into my mouth to match the rhythm of his cock driving into my pussy. With each domineering stroke, he laid claim to everything that I was and offered me himself in return.

"I love you," he promised between kisses, over

and over again. He branded the promise onto my flesh with tongue and teeth.

We came together, our bodies joined as pure bliss sang through our bound souls.

Chapter 12

Massimo

I dropped a kiss on Evelyn's cheek and carefully got out of bed.

"What's wrong?" she murmured, reaching for me in the dark.

I squeezed her hand gently. "Go back to sleep. I need to talk to Gian and Enzo."

My friends had texted me to tell me they were coming to my apartment, and I wanted to fill in some gaps about what'd happened at Evelyn's gallery this afternoon. Enzo had promised to prevent an ensuing war with the Nardone clan, and I had to know that the potential fallout had been handled.

I crossed the bedroom as quietly as I could manage, softly shutting the door behind me so that our conversation wouldn't disturb her.

The brothers were already waiting for me in the kitchen, Gian leaning against the marble topped island while Enzo stood stiffly, uncharacteristic tension gripping his body. Usually, Enzo emanated cool, casual composure. Gian seemed to have loosened his more militant bearing to compensate for his brother's strange mood.

"Is the Nardone situation handled?" I asked.

"We cleaned up the scene and disposed of the bodies," Gian replied. "I don't know how long we have before our rivals notice that some of their men are missing. They will suspect us, especially once they realize you survived Rocco's planned attack." He tipped his chin in my direction. "They know about our deal with the cartels, and they must've decided to go after you as a warning. They realize that their business is in danger, and they want to send a message not to fuck with them."

My fists flexed with the first stirrings of protective violence. "Then if there's war, they will have made the first move. Rocco brought his death upon himself."

Gian shook his head. "I don't want to lose any of our people right now. I meant what I said to Salerno: the Nardone clan will go broke within a year. They'll tear each other apart to fight over the little money that's left. I want us to be whole when the time comes to take out Salerno. We're so close, Massimo."

His eyes shone with a fervent light. He'd bided his time for years, making careful, clandestine moves to overthrow our sadistic boss. If we went to war with our rivals, Salerno would tighten his control over our people to defend our territory. He would consolidate his power at a time when we needed him to become complacent.

I turned my attention to Enzo. "You said you have a plan to avoid a conflict with the Nardone clan."

He offered me a tight nod, his gaze distant, as though he was fixated on something else. "There won't be a war. I'll make sure of it."

"How?" I pressed.

"It's better if you don't know."

I didn't care for his cryptic answer, but I trusted him with my life. He could keep his secrets.

"Thank you," I said to the brothers instead of questioning him. "For cleaning up the mess and for arriving in time to save Evelyn."

"We were worried when you didn't meet us for coffee," Gian replied. "It was a good idea to share the data from her tracker with us."

"What?"

My stomach dropped at Evelyn's soft gasp.

Fuck.

"What are you talking about?" she demanded. "What tracker?"

I turned to find her standing at the threshold to the kitchen. Her delicate features were pinched with suspicion, her willowy body rigid.

"I thought you were asleep," I chided.

She tossed her platinum hair. "So, you thought I wouldn't overhear. I came out here to thank Gian and Enzo for saving me." Her peridot eyes narrowed on me. "Answer me, Massimo. What tracker are you talking about?"

"Nothing that should worry you." I tried to placate her.

"We should go," Gian announced. "I'm glad you're okay, Evelyn."

I closed the distance between my sweet girl and me as the brothers made a quick exit. Her chin tipped back in that defiant posture that set my teeth on edge.

I took a breath and tried to ignore the knots in my stomach. What I'd done was for her own good. She would have to see reason.

"Explain." Her voice was uncharacteristically

terse, and she crossed her arms over her chest in a defensive posture.

"We're both alive because I shared your location with my friends," I told her, keeping my voice as calm as I could manage.

Her lush lips thinned. "How?"

"I don't want to lose you," I hedged. "I swore to protect you, and that meant making sure I can find you if we are ever separated."

"Whatever you've done, it's not good," she said, her voice hitching slightly. "You wouldn't be acting this way if it was. Tell me, Massimo."

My hands settled on her shoulders, anchoring her close to my body. She practically vibrated with tension, and my chest ached at her distress. I'd caused this.

"I injected you with a tracking chip," I admitted, knowing I couldn't lie to her. I would just have to convince her that it'd been the right choice. "My friends arrived in time to save us both because of it. I protected you, just like I promised I would."

All the rosy color drained from her freckled cheeks. "When did you do this to me?"

Her question pierced my heart like a knife. She made it sound like I'd victimized her.

My fingers curved into her shoulders, clutching her to me so that she couldn't recoil in revulsion.

"On the plane from Mexico."

Her eyes darkened with something like betrayal. "That's why you gave me the sleeping pill? You drugged me so that I wouldn't know what you were doing."

"I won't let anyone take you from me," I countered fiercely. "When I thought I lost you in Colombia, it almost drove me insane. You were hurt because I couldn't find you fast enough. I won't allow anything like that to happen ever again."

Tears made her eyes shine. "You should have talked to me about it. You should have asked. You can't keep me in a cage like some pet, Massimo."

"I will do anything to keep you safe." My insides churned, but I couldn't take it back. And I wouldn't remove the tracker. It'd proven its usefulness today. She would have to accept it.

She would have to forgive me.

Her chest convulsed on a shuddering breath. "You told me you were in prison," she reminded me. "You said you never want to be locked up again. Are you going to do the same thing to me?"

My heart twisted. "It's not like that, *farfallina*."

"Isn't it?" she challenged quietly. "You didn't

give me a choice, Massimo. I chose to be with you. I didn't consent to being injected with a tracking chip like a wayward puppy. I'm a person, not a pet."

"You're *mine.*" It was the only explanation I could offer, and the possessive words left me on a low, frustrated growl. "I wasn't living before I met you. I had my friends and our mission, but I was alone, Evelyn. You give my life meaning. I can't live without you. I won't."

Glittering tears spilled down her pale cheeks, and shock tore through me when she placed her hand against my tense jaw.

"I understand that you've had to fight for everything you have," she said quietly. "But I'm not a possession. I need your respect. I'll come to resent you otherwise, and I don't want that. I need you too."

I turned my face and kissed her palm, then sank to my knees before her.

"I do respect you, Evelyn. I love your quiet strength and your fierce devotion. I should've talked to you about the tracker, and I'm sorry for that. But I can't remove it. Think about what happened today. My life is dangerous. You shouldn't be with a man like me, but it's too late to go back now. I can't let you go, and you pledged yourself to me. I love you, *farfallina*. I will never disrespect you like this again, but the tracker stays. I'm sorry. I can live with your resentment, but I can't live without you. Please, forgive me."

She brushed trembling fingers over my furrowed brow. "I love you too." The words were drawn from her like a confession. "I can't live without you either, and I don't want to resent you. I forgive you, but never do anything like this again. It hurts that you did this to me without my consent."

I surged to my feet and wrapped her in a desperate embrace. "I will never cause you pain again," I swore. "I would rather die."

She pressed her cheek to my chest, directly over my racing heart. "It's all right." My sweet girl soothed me. "We'll be okay, Massimo. I'm right here. I'm safe. We're both alive and safe."

I'd committed a grave sin against her, but she was comforting me. I would never deserve this perfect woman, but I was selfish enough to keep her.

"I will make you happy," I swore. "You will have everything you could ever desire."

She peered up at me, gemstone eyes shining. "All I want is you. Being together as equals is all that matters to me. I want to share my life with you as partners."

"You have me," I vowed. "We will never be equals because you are so much better than me, *dolcezza*. You are everything to me."

Her dainty hands bracketed my face. "I love you," she said with the weight of an oath. "You are a good man. I'll tell you every day for the rest of our lives."

I still didn't believe her, but I was hungry to taste the words on her lips. My mouth crashed down on hers, and I staked my selfish claim in a fierce, branding kiss.

Chapter 13

Evelyn

I busied myself in the kitchen, keeping my mind and my hands occupied. Soothing jazz music filled the space, emanating from Massimo's sound system. It provided a calming atmosphere as I took my time chopping fresh tomatoes for a caprese salad.

After our tense conversation about the tracking chip last night, I was anxious to spend more time with him. I wanted to make sure he felt secure in our bond, but he'd left early this morning to see to his business. I'd taken the opportunity to explore the neighborhood with my camera, and I'd discovered a large market nearby; I'd purchased everything that I needed for a romantic evening at home.

I'd spent the late afternoon prepping a sumptuous dinner for us, and I'd decorated the apartment with bouquets of roses. When he returned, we would share a romantic meal, and I would spend hours reassuring him of my love and forgiveness for his transgression against me. I understood that he'd done it out of fear, and Massimo wasn't a man who experienced that emotion often. He was powerful and dangerous, and that unfamiliar fear had clearly driven him to make the wrong decision in his desperation to protect me.

I wouldn't insist that he remove the tracker, but it'd been wrong of him to drug me and inject it without my consent.

But I believed in his contrition, and I was eager to heal the rift between us.

I was so lost in my task and caught up in the music that I didn't hear approaching footsteps.

Corded arms grabbed me from behind, and a strong hand clamped over my mouth, smothering my shocked cry. Something cold and hard pressed against my temple: a gun. A familiar, ocean spray scent surrounded me, and my heart stopped.

George.

My ex-fiancé had come for me.

"I'll make this quick, Evie." His voice was a low and rough with resentment. "You brought this on yourself. It's not what I wanted. I could've made things right between us, but you chose to fuck another man." His fingers bit into my cheeks, his muscles flexing with the force of his possessive rage.

The man I'd once thought I loved was a stranger to me. I'd planned to spend the rest of my life with this monster.

"You thought you could run away to Italy, and I wouldn't follow?" he seethed. "You're supposed to be my wife. But you chose a filthy criminal instead."

My own rage heated my chest. George was corrupt, a criminal himself. He'd been working with a cartel, and he'd proven that he didn't possess the same morals that Massimo lived by. He would've let me die to protect his dirty secret.

"Let her go." The words were a vicious snarl.

My heart leapt into my throat, and George whirled to face the threat. He kept his cruel grip on me, positioning my body in front of his like a shield. The gun remained pressed tightly against my head.

Massimo's silver eyes flashed, and his massive body swelled with protective fury. He held his own gun, but he didn't dare make a move. Not when George could end my life in less than a second.

"Don't come any closer," George snapped, yanking me tight to his chest.

It would be impossible for my Massimo to shoot him without going through me.

I met his flame blue stare, allowing him to look straight into the core of me, to see my love for him. His beautiful features were twisted with rage and terror for me. An odd sense of calm settled over me.

Despite the fact that I faced death, I didn't regret anything that'd happened with the cartels and the Camorra. If I hadn't followed George to Mexico City, I never would've met Massimo.

For years, I'd made myself small for my ex-fiancé. I'd done everything in my power to make him happy, desperate to earn his love in return.

With Massimo, I allowed myself to be difficult at times. I'd challenged him for keeping me against my will, and I stood up to him when he made demands of me that I didn't agree with. I felt empowered to express my full range of emotions with him because I felt inherently safe with my dark protector.

He had offered me his love freely and fiercely.

I opened myself to him, allowing him to see my devotion and gratitude shining through my eyes. No matter what happened now, I wouldn't change one moment we'd shared. He had allowed me to truly be myself for the first time in my life. I would never regret that.

If George to killed me, Massimo would go insane with grief. He might even get shot before my body hit the ground. I wouldn't allow him to be hurt.

And I wouldn't allow George to take one more thing from me, much less my life. I would never make myself small for him ever again.

I reached behind me, and my fingers closed around the knife I'd been using to chop tomatoes. Acting on blind instinct, I stabbed at George's lower back, the awkward angle preventing me from aiming for his black heart.

He screamed and jerked. The gun went off at my ear, deafening at such close range. But there was no pain. My world didn't disappear.

In his moment of agony, his grip had shifted, and the bullet missed me.

I dropped to the tiled floor, denying him the shield of my body. Massimo's gun barked, and George's scream cut off abruptly. He crumpled, his dead weight falling beside me. His familiar, navy-blue eyes stared at me blankly. A gory hole had been torn through the center of his forehead.

Massimo's arms wrapped around me, dragging me away from the man who'd tormented me for years.

My ears rang from the gunshot that'd barely

missed me, so I couldn't make out what my dark savior was saying, but I saw his lips moving as he caressed my face, turning my head to check for signs of injury.

"I'm not hurt." My shaky promise was strangely dull in my head, my hearing temporarily impaired.

He pulled me tightly to his chest, and I felt it rumbling with low, reassuring words I couldn't quite understand. I leaned into him, making reassurances of my own.

My stomach churned in the aftermath of the violence, but I didn't feel remorse over George's death or my role in it. I wouldn't mourn the man who'd betrayed me in the worst way, and I would've done anything to protect Massimo from harm.

"I wouldn't let him take me from you," I said fiercely. "I belong with you, Massimo. I love you."

He lifted me up and carried me out of the kitchen, away from my tormentor's dead body. I closed my eyes and melted into his strong embrace, trusting him to take care of me in every way, just as I would always do everything in my power to protect his heart and mind.

Chapter 14

Massimo

I held Evelyn in our bed while Enzo and Gian cleaned up the bloody mess in the kitchen. A text to my friends was all it took for them to come help me dispose of another body.

No one would know that I'd killed a DEA agent. It was highly unlikely that Crawford had told anyone he was traveling to Italy; he would've kept his plot to eliminate Evelyn secret. As far as the feds were concerned, he would be declared missing in Mexico City. In a few hours, I'd call Carmen and ask for her help framing *Los Zetas*.

The cartel queen would be pleased that Crawford was dead, and it was in her best interest for the DEA to crack down on *Los Zetas*. They'd been brazen enough to attack her home. She would gladly figure out a way to pin Crawford's disappearance on her enemies. Carmen was just as wickedly clever as her husband. She and Duarte would handle it.

My phone buzzed with a message from Gian confirming that my kitchen was now spotless. The brothers had just left my building, giving me complete privacy with my delicate little butterfly.

I cuddled her willowy body, marveling at the precious woman who snuggled into me with such trust and love.

She might be physically delicate, but Evelyn was breathtaking in her quiet strength. She didn't shed so much as a tear over Crawford's death, and in the aftermath, she'd been comforting me as much as I'd been intent on soothing her.

She'd bravely stabbed her ex-fiancé, going against her gentle nature to save us both.

If she'd died, my life would've ceased to have any meaning. Now that I knew the transcendent joy of possessing her good heart, mine couldn't beat without her.

"It's over, *farfallina*," I promised, stroking her silken hair. "You're safe now. You kept us both safe. I'm so proud of you."

She pressed herself closer to me, clinging to me like I was her lifeline. "I couldn't let him hurt you. And I wasn't going to let him hurt me either. Not again. I belong with you, Massimo."

I looked at her with awe. "I will never deserve you, Evelyn. But I will love you and cherish you every day for the rest of our lives."

She trailed her fingers through my curls, her fingernails lightly scraping my scalp in the way that sent pleasant tingles down my spine.

"We deserve each other," she said with quiet intensity. "We both deserve to be happy. I've never had a real family, not in the ways that truly matter. You are my family, Massimo. You've given me the gift of unconditional love. I won't allow anyone to separate us."

I crushed my lips to hers, conveying all of my fierce, possessive, eternal love through the savage kiss. My family had been taken from me when I was a child, my loving parents ripped away on the day Rocco shot them.

He was finally dead, and Evelyn's tormentor had been eliminated too. We were freed from the demons of our pasts. Our shared future opened up before us, full of love and a sense of security I hadn't known since I was a boy. I felt safe with her because I knew she would protect my heart, just as I would do anything to keep her safe. Body, mind, and soul.

We belonged to each other, for the rest of our lives.

Chapter 15

Evelyn

"Isn't it so beautiful?" I gushed, spinning in a circle in an attempt to encompass the stunning villa that was nestled into the side of Capri. It was located on one of the quieter streets above town, so it felt private despite the fact that we were only a fifteen-minute walk from everything we needed. "What do you think?"

"Beautiful," Massimo purred, threading his fingers through my hair and absently rubbing the silken blonde strands.

I giggled and tucked myself closer to his powerful frame. "The villa, Massimo," I reminded him. "It's bigger than what we need, really," I continued, my cheeks warming slightly. "But I thought maybe we might want the extra bedrooms one day."

His silver eyes flashed, and he captured my face in his big hands. "And why is that, *farfallina*?"

We hadn't talked about children yet. My mouth went dry, my anxiety spiking.

"I thought…"

He placed his hand over my heart in a familiar, soothing gesture.

"I want to have a family with you, Massimo," I confessed, calmed by his steady presence. "Is that something you want too?"

He looked at me as though I was his greatest treasure. "More than anything," he rumbled. "We are already a family, Evelyn, but we will grow together. We can live in this villa and wake up to this view every morning with our children."

He turned my body so that I faced away from him, looking out over the infinity pool toward the Faraglioni rock formation where we'd kissed for luck. His big hand splayed over my belly, cradling the place where our child would one day grow.

"If this feels like home, say the word, and it's ours."

I sucked in a deep breath, drinking in the scent of the sea and the rich purple bougainvillea flowers that grew around the patio. It mingled with the scent of leather and amber.

"Yes," I declared, peace settling over me. "This feels like home."

He stepped away, and I mourned the loss of his body heat for only a second before he dropped to one knee before me. A small black jewelry box appeared in his right hand, and he snapped it open to reveal a huge pear-shaped diamond solitaire ring. It matched the shape of my necklace perfectly.

"Be my wife, Evelyn." He slid the ring on my finger before I could fully formulate my reply.

"Yes," I gasped out. "I'm yours, Massimo."

He surged to his feet and swept me up in a devastating kiss. This powerful, dangerous, protective man would be my husband, the father of our children. He was my future. My everything.

He kissed me fiercely, a promise and a slight warning. I belonged to him, and he would never let me go.

I opened for him on a sigh. I was exactly where I wanted to be.

Epilogue

Enzo

Emiliana Rinaldi was as beautiful as I remembered, her long, dark hair framing her fragile features in thick waves. She'd always reminded me of an ethereal creature, a stunning nymph to be coveted; a demigoddess to be worshipped.

My stomach soured.

Not anymore. Once, I'd been utterly devoted to the petite beauty who'd captivated my full attention from the moment I'd seen her all those years ago.

But that was when I was still a stupid, hopeful boy who didn't understand some of the harsher realities of the world. I'd known the Camorra princess was out of my reach, but that hadn't stopped me from grasping for her anyway with grubby, greedy hands.

For a short time, I'd thought she was mine.

I hadn't been this close to her in over a decade. The years had sharpened her features ever so slightly, only enhancing her aura of unearthly beauty rather than diminishing it. Long, thick lashes fanned her high cheekbones, and her lush, rosebud lips were slightly parted in sleep.

For a moment, I simply stared down at her where she lay peacefully in her bed. Once I acted, I wouldn't be able to take it back. I would be bound to her for the rest of my life, no matter if it made us both miserable.

She would be my hostage to prevent war from breaking out with the Nardone clan. Her father would rage when he discovered that I'd taken her, but if I legitimized my claim over her with marriage, they would be coerced into a tense alliance.

Massimo and Gian wouldn't approve of this plan, so I hadn't told them about it. They would have no choice but to accept what I'd done once it was set in motion.

I withdrew the syringe from my pocket and silently stalked toward my unwilling bride.

Thank you for reading ENDLESS OBSESSION! I hope you loved Massimo and Evelyn's story. Enzo's dark romance is up next in PRINCE OF RUIN.

Did you know that KING OF RUIN is a spin-off of the Captive Series? Dive into this world of dangerous antiheroes who will do anything to possess the women they love. It all starts when cartel kingpin Andrés captures FBI agent Samantha in SWEET CAPTIVITY.

Turn the page for an explosive excerpt...

Sweet Captivity Excerpt

"You don't want to do this," I choked out past the lump of terror that clogged my throat. I kept a wary eye on the wicked hunting knife Cristian Moreno held naturally at his side, as though it were an innocuous extension of his arm rather than a threat to my life. "Let me go."

He threw back his head and laughed, his perfect white teeth flashing as the booming sound assaulted my eardrums. My hands shook violently, causing the ropes that bound my arms behind me to chafe against my wrists. The burn of the rough fibers against my skin and cold bite of the metal chair beneath me were peripheral; my entire focus was centered on Moreno and the way the gleam of the spare overhead light bulb made his dark eyes glint as sharply as the knife in his hand.

"No, Samantha," he corrected me calmly, his light Colombian accent making his deep voice almost lyrical when he spoke my name. "You're never leaving this place. Not alive, at least. If you answer my questions, I might be inclined to mercy. Otherwise..." He left the unspoken threat hanging in the air, the implication clear. I would experience agony before he finally disposed of me.

No. Don't think like that.

I gasped in several deep breaths so I could manage to speak again.

"My friends will find me," I asserted, knowing Dex wouldn't leave me to die here. My best friend would do whatever it took to rescue me.

"If they do, they won't find more than what's left of your body."

Ice crystallized in my veins. He took a step toward me, raising the knife. I tried to shrink away, but the unyielding metal chair behind my back kept me immobile.

"You can't hurt me," I said desperately, twisting against my restraints. "If you kill me, my friends will hunt you down."

His dazzling smile illuminated his darkly handsome features with cruel amusement.

"I want them to know what I've done. Your death will be a warning. We're going to send a little message to your friends." He gestured behind him, and for the first time, my gaze darted away from the threat before me.

A man loomed a few feet away, the light on his smart phone indicating that he was recording me. A wicked scar puckered his tanned cheek, deepening his fearsome scowl. His black gaze bored into me, his dark glare penetrating my soul. I shuddered and tore my eyes away, unable to bear looking at him.

Moreno laughed again. "What, you don't like my little brother?" He cocked his head at me. "Maybe I'll give you to him to play with, after I'm finished with you. He has... very *unique* tastes." He reached for me, his long fingers trailing down my cheek. I cringed away, my stomach churning. "I think Andrés will like you. Such pale skin. It will mark up nicely." He shook his head slightly, still smiling. "But I'm getting ahead of myself. He can have you when I'm done. I'm going to extract my answers first."

The sharp knife kissed my throat, and I choked on a scream as horror overwhelmed me.

Cristian stepped behind me so his brother's camera could get clearer footage of what I was enduring. His big fist tangled in my hair, jerking my head back so I had no choice but to stare up into his cruel black eyes.

The cold tip of the knife scraped upward from the center of my throat, grazing over my skin as it traced a path under my chin. I stopped breathing when the flat of the blade swiped across the line of my lips. A high whimper slipped through them, the resultant vibration threatening to make the knife pierce my skin. As it was, the tightly packed nerve endings on my lips sparked as the cool metal kissed them.

The knife left my mouth, but I didn't have time to suck in a panting breath before the frigid blade returned to my throat.

"You were in my territory today, watching my people. One of my men followed you home. Who are you working for?" he demanded.

"I'm FBI," I said, my voice barely more than a whisper. With the knife at my throat, I could scarcely draw the breath I needed to speak.

He frowned at me. "A sniper made an attempt on my life a few days ago. The feds wouldn't assassinate me. Who are you really working for?" The blade sliced a thin, stinging line across my throat.

"I really am FBI," I said in a rush, the truth spilling from my lips. If he knew I was a federal agent, he wouldn't dare hurt me. "My name is Samantha Browning. I'm a tech analyst. Well, I was. I'm a field agent now. I'm not trying to kill you. We're investigating you. You have to know you're on our radar. Please, I swear I'm FBI." I was aware that I was babbling, but I couldn't stop pleading for my life.

He considered me for a long, terrifying moment, weighing my fate. "You're a tech analyst? That means you have access to all the evidence the feds have on me. If you're telling the truth about who you are."

"I am," I said quickly. "You can't hurt me. If you do, my friends will come after you."

"I think I'll give you to my brother, after all," he mused. "He'll make sure you're telling the truth. I'd rather not mutilate you, if you're going to be useful to me. Andrés has more creative ways of breaking women. And I'll keep our little video to ourselves. If you are who you say you are, I'd rather your friends at the FBI didn't know I have you."

The knifepoint pressed against my cheek, just

below my left eye. The pressure increased slightly, and I felt warmth bead on my skin. It slid down my cheek like a crimson tear. My eyes watered, and Cristian's handsome face wavered above me.

"Maybe I'll give you a scar to match my brother's first," he mused.

A deep growl sounded from a few feet in front of me, and I knew it came from Andrés. I couldn't so much as glance in his direction; Cristian's long fingers in my hair kept me immobile.

A sharp grin lit his features with amusement. "Apparently, he wants you mostly intact. Should I give him what he wants?"

The fearsome growl sounded again, a wordless warning. I shuddered, equally as frightened of the prospect of his desire to *have me* as I was of the knife piercing my cheek.

"Not the face, then," Cristian said decisively. "But I think I'll let Andrés see what he's getting to work with."

The knife left my face, but the blade instantly hooked beneath the top button of my shirt. It gave way easily as the sharp steel tore through thread. He continued to move the blade downward, trailing a sickening path between my breasts, over my navel, down to the top of my slacks. The fabric fell open with a flick of the knife, leaving me exposed in my white cotton bra.

A plea for mercy locked in my throat. I couldn't speak, could barely breathe. My mind began to shut down, the adrenaline created by fear clouding my brain.

Cristian's fingers tightened in my hair, giving me a bite of pain. "Stay with us, Samantha," he ordered smoothly.

The world sharpened around me with cruel clarity just before pain sliced into me. The tip of the knife grated a torturously slow line along my right collarbone. The cut was shallow, but blood welled up as the blade scraped bone. The scream that had been trapped inside me burst out as pain seared through me. He hooked the blade beneath the little strip of cotton at the middle of my bra, parting the fabric and exposing me.

My scream choked off on a sob as terror mingled with humiliation.

"What do you think, *hermanito*?" Cristian asked with mild interest. "Is she pretty enough for you? She's not a great beauty, but her nipples stand out nicely against her pale skin."

My skin turned frigid, my flesh pebbling as ice sank into my veins. I vaguely recognized that I was going into shock as my entire body began to shake violently.

"And her eyes are quite lovely," he continued in detached observation. "So much fear there. You like when they're frightened, don't you, Andrés?"

His low grunt in reply rolled around my mind, but my capacity for conscious thought had been ripped to shreds. The knife left my breasts to slice through the ropes that bound my wrists behind me. I slumped forward, my watery muscles incapable of holding me upright.

Strong arms closed around my shoulders, bracing me before I slid to the floor. I was dimly aware of my body being lifted. My head lolled back, and the last thing I saw before my mind short-circuited was Andrés' fearsome, scarred face looming over me.

Stinging pain on my chest yanked me back to awareness, and I bolted upright with a gasp. Panic blinded me, but firm hands gripped my upper arms, pressing me back down against something soft that cushioned my body. I was no longer sitting on the unyielding metal chair. I recognized the feel of a mattress beneath me, and my torso was pinned down against it by a strong, masculine hold.

I squirmed and kicked, instinctively trying to fight my way free. I became aware of cool air against my breasts, and I realized I was still exposed. My heart hammered against my ribcage, and I doubled my efforts to fight off the man holding me down, my fingers clawing blindly. His hands easily encircled my wrists, trapping them at either side of my hips.

"Calm down, *cosita*, or I'll have to restrain you." I recognized the soft Colombian accent.

Moreno had me. He'd hurt me, stripped me...

Oh god. He'd given me to his terrifying brother. Andrés.

And now I was half-naked and helpless in his steely hold.

I couldn't stop thrashing, my muscles rippling with effort to break free. My stomach twisted, nausea rising as the full horror of my situation came down on me.

A low sound of disapproval grated against my mind. His grip instantly shifted, tugging my arms over my head. He secured them there with one big hand. Something cool and supple encircled my right wrist. Metal jingled against metal as he buckled the cuff into place.

I twisted my entire body, trying to angle myself so I could kick out at him. Desperation clawed at my insides, and all my training left my head as animal terror took hold. My awkward attempts to resist him made no effect, and he quickly secured my other wrist.

Working in silence, he caught my left ankle, pulling it diagonally toward the bottom corner of the bed. My eyes finally focused and I watched in helpless horror as he bound my legs to either side of the four-poster, spreading me wide. I still wore my slacks, but I felt terribly exposed and vulnerable.

I thrashed against the restraints, but he pressed his big palm against my bare abdomen, pinning me down against the mattress and effectively ending my struggles. All I could do was jerk uselessly against the cuffs. Fear coursed through me. My fight-or-flight instincts had settled on flight, but there was nowhere for me to go. That didn't stop my body from twisting like a wild thing, panic beating against the inside of my chest.

His dark eyes watched me with calm certainty as he simply waited. I wasn't sure how long it took for my muscles to burn with exertion, and I finally gave up, my limbs trembling where they were stretched above and below me, laying me out before him.

"Are you done?" he asked coolly.

"Fuck you," I seethed, my acid tongue the only weapon left to me.

Keeping me pinned in place with one hand, his other swiftly came down and cracked across the outer swell of my breasts, one after the other in rapid succession. My sensitive flesh instantly began to burn, and I cried out. I couldn't escape the pain; I was trapped in place for the harsh censure.

Tears leaked from the corners of my eyes, and he finally stopped.

"I won't tolerate insults," he said, still unnervingly calm. It almost would have been less disconcerting if he'd shouted. "You will speak to me with respect. Do you understand?"

"No." The refusal came out as a horrified moan.

"You will understand soon," he said, utterly confident. "You're frightened, but you will learn. For now, I'm warning you not to curse at me again. Tell me you'll obey."

The tears came faster, spilling down my temples and falling into my hair.

His face shifted to a forbidding mask. "Tell me."

I couldn't manage more than a fearful whimper, but I nodded shakily. I didn't want him to slap me again, and I recognized that there was nothing I could do to prevent him from doing it if he decided he wanted to.

His countenance softened, his scar easing so it wasn't as pronounced. "In the future, I will expect a verbal answer. You belong to me now, Samantha. Defiance will lead to punishment. Obedience will be rewarded. You choose whichever you want. I might seem like a harsh Master, but I'm fair. Your behavior has consequences, either painful or pleasurable for you."

"Please," I forced out past the lump in my throat. "I can't... I don't... Don't..." I began to pant out the fragmented words as my breathing turned shallower, until I was gasping but not drawing in air.

His hands bracketed my face, shockingly gentle. "Breathe," he ordered, his accented voice low and soft, as though trying to soothe a frightened animal.

I certainly felt like a panicked, primal thing; trapped and terrified.

His fingers threaded through my hair on either side of my head, massaging gently.

"Breathe with me," he cajoled. He drew in a slow, deep breath and then blew it out on a long exhale. "Again," he commanded, and I vaguely recognized that I'd obeyed and matched his breathing, my lungs too desperate for oxygen to resist. I sucked in another shaky breath, mirroring him. We repeated the process several more times, until I was able to breathe almost normally. I sank down into the mattress as my body went limp, all the fight going out of me as exhaustion sapped my mind.

"Better." He nodded his approval. His gaze finally diverted from my face, and he reached for a damp cloth that he'd placed beside me on the bed. "You're still bleeding," he told me. "I'm going to clean you up. This will sting a little. Stay still."

I couldn't have moved away even if I still possessed any willpower to do so. One of his hands remained bracketed at the side of my face, his thumb hooking beneath my jaw to hold me steady.

The cool cloth gently touched my cheek, and I hissed in pain. Just as he'd warned me, the solution that soaked the cloth stung, and I knew it was more than water.

"Good girl," he said, the warm praise in his tone fucking with my addled mind. I only recognized the comfort in it, unable to process the twisted nature of how he was manipulating me. Anything was preferable to the unrelenting terror that had utterly sapped my will and smothered all thought of resistance.

He continued his gentle ministrations, his dark eyes completely focused on his task as he cleaned the cut on my collarbone. Keening sounds eased up my throat, and he softly shushed me.

When he finished, he sat back and considered me for a long moment, his black eyes searching mine. Instinct urged me to look away, to escape his probing gaze. The intensity with which he watched me made it impossible for me to break eye contact. I shuddered violently, unable to bear his scrutiny.

His grip on my face shifted, and his calloused fingertips smoothed over the furrow in my brow.

"You're hurting," he remarked. "You didn't do anything to deserve this."

He reached for something else on the bed beside me, and I cringed when my gaze fixed on it: a syringe. I didn't want to be unconscious again, helpless and unable to defend myself.

"My brother gave me this in case I needed to subdue you, but it will take away your pain. I told you, I'm a fair Master. I won't hurt you if you don't earn a punishment."

"I don't want it," I managed to whisper.

"I decide what's best for you from now on," he declared calmly.

"Please," I begged uselessly as he carefully slid the needle into my arm.

"Hush now, *cosita*," he murmured. "You'll feel better when you wake up."

"No," I slurred, the drugs making my tongue heavy within seconds.

His long fingers smoothed over my hair, petting me as I fell into darkness.

Also by Julia Sykes

The Captive Series

Sweet Captivity

Claiming My Sweet Captive

Stealing Beauty

Captive Ever After

Pretty Hostage

Wicked King

Ruthless Savior

Eternally His

King of Ruin

Tainted Obsession

Illicit Obsession

Endless Obsession

The Impossible Series

Impossible

Savior

Rogue

Knight

Mentor

Master

King

A Decadent Christmas (An Impossible Series Christmas Special)

Czar

Crusader

Prey (An Impossible Series Short Story)

Highlander

Decadent Knights (An Impossible Series Short Story)

Centurion

Dex

Hero

Wedding Knight (An Impossible Series Short Story)

Valentines at Dusk (An Impossible Series Short Story)

Nice & Naughty (An Impossible Series Christmas Special)

Dark Lessons

Mafia Ménage Trilogy

Mafia Captive

The Daddy and The Dom

Theirs to Protect

Their Captive Bride

In Their Hands

In Their Power

In Their Hearts

Fallen Mafia Prince Trilogy

Fallen Prince

Stolen Princess

Fractured Kingdom

Printed in Great Britain
by Amazon